Choices

She was only seventeen, with her whole life ahead of her. Uni, friends, travel ... and pregnancy.

It was so unfair. They'd only done it a few times and it hadn't even been that good. Not like it was in books or movies. And now she had to make a choice, and live with the consequences.

Dianne Wolfer lives in a seaside town on the south coast of Western Australia, but has also lived for extensive periods in Japan, Thailand and Nepal. She has published two previous novels for young adults, *Dolphin Song* (1996) and *Border Line* (1998).

Choices

Choices

Dianne Wolfer

FREMANTLE ARTS CENTRE PRESS

First published 2001 by
FREMANTLE ARTS CENTRE PRESS
25 Quarry Street, Fremantle
(PO Box 158, North Fremantle 6159)
Western Australia.
www.facp.iinet.net.au

Consultant Editor Alwyn Evans.
Production Coordinator Cate Sutherland.
Cover Designer Marion Duke.
Typeset by Fremantle Arts Centre Press
and printed by Australian Print Group.

National Library of Australia
Cataloguing-in-publication data

Wolfer, Dianne.
Choices

ISBN 1 86368 317 8.

1. Teenage pregnancy – Juvenile fiction. I. Title.

A823.3

The State of Western Australia has made an investment in this project
through ArtsWA in association with the Lotteries Commission.

Publication of this title was assisted by the Commonwealth Government
through the Australia Council, its arts funding and advisory body.

for
Sophie, Tolina and Karen

Acknowledgements

I would like to thank Moira Brodie and members of kaleidoscope (SWW magazine group) for their support and feedback from the earliest stages of *Choices*. Shelly Hayes' advice regarding relinquishing mothers/children was much appreciated, as was Geoff Havel's help talking through the introduction of the character Jacinta. Thanks to Lil and Becky Dore for reading an early draft, to Anne Peachey, Tracey Lawrie and also to friends who shared their own birth stories. It made writing the '39 weeks' chunk lots of fun!

Thank you to all at Fremantle Arts Centre Press, especially Alwyn Evans for her insightful and patient editing skills.

I hope this story will help young men and women make choices that are right for them.

Dianne Wolfer

'Go on, girl, you can do it.
It's only life,
there's nothing to it.'

(lyrics from a Marcia Hines song)

Prologue

Elisabeth's hand trembled as she lifted the jar of warm liquid. She wanted to run away and scream that it was all a mistake, but instead she took a deep breath and poured her urine over the plastic pregnancy tester. A few drops spilt on the bathroom tiles.

She shivered. It was so unfair. They'd only done it a few times and it hadn't even been that good. Not like it was in books or movies. She looked at her watch and crossed her fingers as her brother rattled the door handle.

'I'm busy!' she yelled.

'All right, keep your hair on.' He walked away. Then, the blue lines appeared. Elisabeth stared at the tester and knew that now she had to make a choice.

PART ONE

Libby: 5 weeks

Libby sat on a rock staring out to sea. She loved Darren, but did she want to spend the rest of her life with him? For weeks she'd been trying to imagine a forty-year-old Darren. His dad was balding, one of those comb-the-strands-over-the-head blokes, and he drank too much. Darren drank too, but he usually kept it under control. Would he always?

The idea of waking up next to Darren bothered her the most. Libby's bed was her refuge, a space for dreams. Having him there permanently would be suffocating.

Libby wondered if she could go through with it on her own. Images of single mums crowded her brain – all of them negative. She wondered how her friends would react and wished she could talk it over with Ashleigh. Then she thought about school, the exams and her music. A baby would mean giving all that up. But what else could she do?

Libby had tried to convince herself that having an abortion would be easier. No one would ever know, but she couldn't do it. The tiny blob of cells dividing in her belly held life. Only God could take that. And Libby didn't think she'd be able to give up a baby for adoption, so that left only one choice.

An ant crawled over the rock beside her. Libby held

her finger above it. She could kill it, or let it live. Just as she had power over the creature sustaining itself through a cord in her belly. She shivered. This decision would affect the rest of her life.

And what about its father? Beth remembered Darren's panic-stricken face when she'd told him her period was late.

'Sorry, Darren,' she whispered, 'but it's my body. This has to be *my* choice.'

Libby stood up. She took a deep breath and watched the ant scurry to safety.

Beth: 6 weeks

Beth sat on a rock staring out to sea. She loved Darren, but did she want to spend the rest of her life with him? For weeks she'd been trying to imagine a forty-year-old Darren. His dad was balding, one of those comb-the-strands-over-the-head blokes, and he drank too much. Darren drank too, but he usually kept it under control. Would he always?

The idea of waking up next to Darren bothered her the most. Beth's bed was her refuge, a space for dreams. Having him there permanently would be suffocating.

Beth wondered if she could go through with it on her own. Was she strong enough to become a single mum? She kept seeing images of nappies, vomit and a flabby belly. They didn't fit her plans for playing cello and travelling. But if becoming a seventeen-year-old mother wasn't the right path for her, what else could she do? Beth didn't think she'd be able to give up a baby for adoption, so that left only one choice.

She blocked the memory of her gurgling baby cousin. The clump of cells nestling in her womb wasn't like that. It wasn't anything like a baby. Not yet. But it was growing all the time. Soon its seahorse tail would become a backbone, and arm buds would develop into limbs. She remembered the photos in Ashleigh's

13

Human Biology book and knew she had to decide soon.

An ant crawled over the rock beside her. Beth held her finger above it. She could kill it, or let it live. Just as she had power over the creature sustaining itself through a cord in her belly.

'You have to decide today,' she muttered.

Beth hummed a few bars of the cello piece she was learning and stared out to sea. She thought about her parents and Father Patrick, but there was no point asking their advice. Beth knew she couldn't go through with this pregnancy. She wasn't ready to be a mother. Not yet. Not when her life was just beginning. But was it fair to put her needs first? Beth sighed. Maybe it was selfish, but she couldn't give up her dreams. Besides, a baby deserved a mother who could give love unconditionally.

And what about its father? Beth remembered Darren's panic-stricken face when she'd told him her period was late.

'Sorry, Darren,' she whispered, 'but it's my body. This has to be *my* choice.'

Beth stood up. She took a deep breath, ground the ant into the rock and went home to make an appointment.

Libby: 7 weeks

Libby's days began at six o'clock when she scurried to the toilet to vomit. One morning her mother was waiting outside the door with a glass of water.

'When's it due?' she asked. Libby burst into tears. 'Blow your nose,' Gail said, fishing in her dressing-gown pockets for a tissue. 'Crying won't make it disappear. We need to talk.' Libby filled the tissue and stared at the floor. 'I s'pose it's Darren's,' her mother continued.

Libby nodded. She felt numb, as if her mind was floating above them. She tried to concentrate on her mother's words, but the surreal atmosphere only thickened.

'Does Darren know?'

'Not yet.'

'Have you been to the doctor?'

Libby shook her head. 'I don't need to.' She showed her mother the tester and they stared at the thin, blue lines.

'Well,' Gail said at last. 'So much for going to university next year.'

'Is that all you can think of?'

'What do you want me to say?'

Libby wanted to cry, but her mother's fierce tone froze her sobs, making them sink back and settle like dead meat in her belly. 'Aren't you disappointed?' she mumbled.

'Of course I'm disappointed, Elisabeth. Aren't you? But telling you off would make me a hypocrite wouldn't it?' Libby nodded, but didn't guess what her mother meant. She hugged her arms to her chest and winced. Her breasts were so sore.

'Well,' Gail said. 'We'd better ring Dr Fitzpatrick. Get dressed while I make an appointment.'

Libby changed into jeans and a T-shirt, then made a cup of weak tea.

'She can't see you until ten thirty. I'll have to drop off the flowers for church on the way. Do you want to help me in the garden, or have you got homework?'

'I'll work on my English essay.'

'Right.' Gail took a bucket and her secateurs and strode out the back door. After a few moments Libby's brother wandered in. He grunted in her direction then shook a massive serve of iron-man food into his bowl. Wishful thinking, she thought, looking at his lanky, puppy body.

'Close the door after you,' she snapped. 'It's cold.'

'Yeah, all right. Any more milk in the fridge?'

Libby passed him a carton and listened to the buzz of her father's shaver whining along the hallway. The thought of her dad knowing made Libby's stomach turn. She tried to swallow some toast but it stuck in her throat.

'How come you've got your jeans on?' her brother asked.

'I feel sick,' Libby said, sipping her tea.

'You don't look sick.'

Libby ignored him as their father rushed in, smelling like a pine forest.

'Morning,' he said. 'Hey, what's up, Libby? No school today?'

'She's sick,' James muttered through a mouthful of cereal.

'Nothing serious?'

'Just queasy,' Libby croaked, trying to wet her mouth.

'Well, I've gotta go. First job's at nine. *I'm off now, Gail,*' he shouted through the screen door. 'I'll pick up the meat on my way home.'

Gail waved her secateurs. 'Chicken breasts,' she yelled. 'Make sure he doesn't give you wings again.'

'Okay.' Jim grabbed his keys, then kissed Libby's head. 'Get better, Princess,' he whispered. Libby nodded and dropped her toast into the compost bucket. She stood by the window watching her mother dead-head the daisies and wished she could disappear.

Beth: 8 weeks

Beth wagged school on the third Friday in June and caught a bus to the clinic across the city. She still hadn't told Darren, and her best friend, Ashleigh, wasn't speaking to her, so although they'd told her to bring someone, Beth went alone.

A herd of pro-lifers was circling the entrance, and Beth realised she'd have to push through them to get inside. There was a driveway beside the clinic. Alongside the driveway was a service station. If she jumped the fence, she could try and nick in before they saw her. Or maybe it would be better to wait until they left.

Beth glanced at her watch. Nine thirty. If she was late, they might reschedule her. Send her away. That would be ten times worse than running past a group of fanatics. *Fanatics*, she reminded herself. That's all they are. Why should I care what they think? It's my body and my decision. She repeated the words as she crossed the road. 'My body, my decision. My body, my decision.'

The service station was quiet. Beth bought some lifesavers from the bored attendant, then strolled towards the fence. She was in luck. The crossbeams were on her side. Beth stepped onto the first beam, took a deep breath, then hurled herself over the fence. She pushed through the shrubs and ran towards the clinic door. The protesters spotted her, and one howled in frustration. He ran up and shoved the bloodied image of a foetus at her face, until his mate whistled him back.

'Gabriel. Out,' he yelled. 'Quick, man, out of their yard.'

'Baby killer,' Gabriel hissed. He spat at her then ran back to the mob. Beth slammed the door behind her and flopped onto a chair. She wiped Gabriel's spit off her shoe. She was panting, but dizzy with relief that she'd made it. The termination would go ahead. Nothing else mattered.

'Are you okay?'

Beth looked around. She hadn't noticed the nurse behind the reception bench.

'Yeah, I guess so. I'm Sally,' she lied, passing over her cousin's Medicare card. 'Sally Jones.'

'Right then, Sally. We've received your referral. Our counsellor's expecting you. I'm sorry about that.' She waved her hand outside. 'Some days are worse than others. Now, if you could just fill in these forms, we'll have a quick check-up and chat in the consulting room.'

Beth's skin prickled. 'What,' she tried to say, but her mouth was dry. 'What … are they for?'

'The forms? Oh, just routine,' the nurse smiled. 'Doctor needs to know if you're allergic to anything.'

'I'm not,' Beth said.

'Good, well then, just fill in the forms, dear. And we'll need a signature at the bottom.'

The pen slipped from her sweaty hands and Beth almost vomited as she bent to pick it up. She looked around. Someone was watching her. The other girl in the waiting room was young, but her eyes weren't. Wise in a tired way, she had the world-weary look of kids on the news. Kids caught in wars they didn't understand.

Beth held the pen, ready to sign her cousin's name, but writing a false name made her hesitate. As if she was formalising the lie. Giving it life. Am I doing the right thing? she wondered again. Then she thought about the rock by the sea. I need to give my dreams a chance, she reminded herself. I can't bring a child into this world until I know I can look after it and give it the unconditional love it deserves.

The protesters began chanting again. Their slogans seeped into the room.

'Abortion is murder. Save the babies. Murder the murderers!' Beth shuddered. Were they allowed to say those things?

The nurse turned up the music, but not before the other girl started sniffling.

'Your turn, Marina,' the nurse said gently. Marina flinched. 'Have you changed your mind? Do you need more time?'

'No, it's just those people outside. They told me it's a sin. That what I'm doing is wicked. They pushed blood-spattered things at me. Things they use to kill babies.'

'It's okay. Take a deep breath. They say those things to upset you. It's part of their tactics. Just take a deep breath. That's it. Don't let them frighten you.' She took the girl's hand and led her, milky-faced and trembling, behind a partition in the corner. 'Only you can make this decision, Marina,' the nurse said, 'and if you've changed your mind, it's okay …'

'No! Of course not,' Marina snapped. 'As if I'd want *this* child! It's just … Can't you get rid of them? I couldn't bear going past them again. Not later, not after …'

'I'm sorry, Marina, as long as they stay outside the gate, we can't do a thing about it.'

'But they said they'd follow me. Get my name.'

'They can't do that.'

'But they said …'

'They said they could, but they can't.'

'What about when that doctor was charged? They had names then.'

'But they didn't make them public. If they'd done that, they would have been taken to court.'

'They still had them.'

'We lock our records, Marina. You don't have to worry. Please believe that. Now, you said that your sister is coming to take you home?' There was a muffled reply. Beth felt bad eavesdropping but she couldn't stop herself.

'Well then, she can park at the back. We'll help you to her car afterwards and that'll be the end of it. Okay?' She led the girl to a chair near Beth and smiled.

'Okay,' she repeated. 'Feeling better?' Marina nodded, but she still looked shaky. 'Now, wait here and I'll see if the counsellor is ready.'

Despite the blaring meditation music, the room seemed quiet after she'd gone. Beth snuck a sideways look at the girl.

'Bastards, pricks, bastards,' she heard her mutter. 'They should parade in front of my uncle's office, not here.'

Her uncle's office? It took Beth a moment to realise what she meant. Then she glanced at the girl again. She looked barely sixteen. Beth felt she should say something, show solidarity. Show her that she understood. But she didn't understand. Marina might be a victim, but Beth couldn't blame anyone. It was her fault, hers and Darren's, that she was here.

'Shame! Shame! Shame!' The pro-lifers had raised their voices. Beth wondered whether knowing Marina's story would soften their rage. Probably not. She'd read too many 'Letters to the Editor' in the Catholic newspaper to believe those extremists capable of compassion. The rights of incest victims were less than an embryo's. That was the bottom line. Beth shook her head. Her mind was a mess. Thoughts wobbled about like jelly in a trifle.

**

'Sally Jones,' the nurse called. Beth stood up. 'Doctor Spagnoli is ready for your procedure-counselling session.'

'Sit down here, Sally,' the counsellor began, 'I'm Lucia Spagnoli. You can call me Lucia or Doctor, whichever you prefer.'

Doctor Lucia talked about the hundreds of couples waiting to adopt babies and told Beth about girls who'd coped with support from their families. *As if I haven't thought about those options*, Beth felt like yelling, but she listened quietly. Then Doctor Lucia discussed future contraception.

'I've decided to keep away from boys,' Beth said.

'Well, best to know, just in case ...' Finally Doctor Lucia explained what was about to happen. Step-by-step.

Beth could choose whether to have a local anaesthetic and be aware of the doctor's suction instruments, or be sedated intravenously and wake up when it was all over. The thought of watching someone remove the cell mass which would never develop into a baby gave Beth the creeps. Even though it looked more alien than human at this stage, it was sharing her blood and oxygen, and it did contain the building blocks of a baby.

'I'd like intravenous sedation,' Beth said. Nausea afterwards was a small price to pay for ignorance. Doctor Spagnoli patted Beth's arm then led her back to the waiting room.

'Not long now,' she said. Beth watched the pro-lifers circling and shuddered. Why did they have to make it worse?

**

When she came to, Beth felt like her insides had been ripped out, and maybe they had. Maybe something more than physical had also been removed.

'Hello, Sally.' The nurse was smiling at her. Sally? Who was Sally?

'I need to …' Beth leant over the trolley bed and tried to vomit. But all that came out was watery dribble. She gagged, then dry-retched, until she felt the back of her throat cramp.

'There now, you'll feel better soon.'

But she didn't. Her belly ached. Beth tried to fold into a foetal position to ease the cramps, but that was worse. She wished Ashleigh was with her. If only she hadn't called Spud a Neanderthal …

'It hurts,' she moaned.

'I know, dear. Try to be brave and rest for a while.'

Someone wheeled her into a recovery cubicle and Beth caught a glimpse of Marina's face in the opposite room. She looked away, feeling like she'd trespassed on the other girl's soul. It was as if someone had peeled away Marina's everyday mask. Her expression was so raw and honest.

The silence from the other cubicle strangled Beth's sniffling. If that young girl could bear it, then so could she. Beth wondered whether Marina's parents knew about the abortion, and whether anything would happen to her uncle. A stabbing pain cut into her thoughts and she let herself drift into a weird semi-sleep.

Heels click-clacking along the corridor roused her. She listened as someone whispered to Marina. Her sister perhaps. Then she looked at the clock. Twenty past two. Time to go. Beth rolled over and moaned. She'd had no idea it would ache like this. How on earth would she get home?

The nurse came in and gave Beth a smile. 'You've got some colour back in your cheeks,' she said before taking her blood pressure and checking her pad. 'Now, who did you say was picking you up?'

'No one,' Beth muttered. 'No one's coming. I'll catch a taxi.'

The nurse frowned. 'But I must have told you on the phone … We like our patients to be accompanied. Are you sure I can't call anyone.'

'No, please just call me a cab.'

'Will there be someone at home?'

'Yes, of course,' Beth lied. She'd chosen a Friday

because her parents would be late. Her mother's landscaping class didn't finish until six, and her dad would be watching James' footy team lose again. She'd have time to get home and be brave. Whatever happened, they mustn't guess. She couldn't bear their disappointment.

'Well, if you're sure,' the nurse said, 'but I'd like you to ring when you get home, so that I know everything's okay.' Beth nodded and struggled to sit up. The room spun around, then up and down. She felt like a horse on a merry-go-round. Beth closed her eyes, almost expecting to hear the brash whistle of a calliope. Instead, she heard Marina and her sister drive away.

'Are you sure you're okay?' Beth nodded and tried to forget the peeled-mask face of Marina. She took a deep breath and hoped the uncle would be punished.

A taxi pulled into the driveway. 'Don't forget to phone,' the nurse said.

'Okay.' Beth thanked her and waddled out alone, feeling braver now that the protesters had gone. As she hobbled to the kerb, Beth felt clumps of herself drip onto the thick sanitary napkin in her underpants. Clumps of her childhood, and the short pleasure of her time with Darren. Clumps of trust. Clumps of honesty. Clumps of faith.

The woozy feeling continued as they drove through the city. Beth bit her cheek and forced herself to chat with the driver. He sized her up in the mirror and answered slowly. She knew that he knew what kind of clinic it was, but she had to be strong. She still had to face her parents and pretend. Beth asked the driver to stop at the corner. Somehow she'd walk the last twenty metres.

Darren was sitting under a tree in her front yard. He put out his hand to help her, but Beth shook him off.

'You weren't at school. Is everything ... umm, okay?' he asked.

'It will be from now on,' she replied.

'Do you need money?'

'I don't know what you mean,' Beth hissed. 'Why would I need money? I told you. My period was late, but everything's fine now. It was probably that flu I had. They reckon that can delay it ...'

Darren stared at the ground. She could see he didn't believe her, and although he didn't say anything Beth knew he was relieved. Suddenly she despised him. Darren reached out to hold her hand. 'I'm sorry,' he began, but Beth pulled away.

'I'm late, I'd better go,' she said. 'See you.' After stumbling inside, Beth rang the clinic then collapsed onto her bed. She stared at the crucifix above her bed until it dissolved intothe evening shadows. When her parents came home and found her in the dark, she said she had a headache.

'Another one?' her dad asked. 'Perhaps you're overdoing the studies. It's going to be a tough year, Princess. You need to pace yourself.' Beth nodded and walked slowly towards the bathroom, worried that jerky movements would bring on more bleeding.

'Darling, your eyes are red. I really think we should make an appointment at the optometrists ...'

'Mum, my eyes are fine. I'm just tired!'

'All right, Elisabeth, there's no need to snap. Do you want something to eat?'

'I'll be okay. I just need to rest,' Beth shouted. Her parents exchanged glances then took their wine glasses into the lounge room. When Beth heard them turn on the news, she went back to bed, buried her head under a pillow and sobbed until she fell asleep.

**

On Monday, Beth found an envelope with a hundred and fifty dollars in her school bag. A note was paper-clipped to the money: *Can we talk?*

But Beth didn't want to talk. She just wanted to put the experience behind her.

Darren had a job stacking trolleys. Beth knew he'd been saving for a wetsuit. She threw away the note and kept the money. He could afford to suffer.

When Darren rang, Beth told her parents she didn't want to talk to him. 'We've broken up,' she said. Then she went to her room and plucked at her cello. Gail waited five minutes before knocking at her door.

'I'm sorry, darling,' her mother murmured, as she perched on the end of her bed. 'I remember my first boyfriend. He said he loved me, then went off with my best friend.' Beth felt like screaming. If only it were that simple.

'I could never understand why he did that,' her mother continued. 'Why not just tell me he wanted to end things, and then go out with Deidre?'

Beth put down her cello, interested despite herself. 'What did you do?' she asked.

Gail laughed. 'The usual things. First I cried. Then I ranted and raved. Then I got over him.' She smiled at Beth. 'Is that what happened with you and Darren?' Beth hesitated. She longed to tell someone. To be absolved. Have someone reassure her that she'd done the right thing. But her mother would have a fit if she knew the truth. Abortion was a mortal sin.

'Something like that,' Beth muttered at last.

'Well, if you want to talk about it ...'

'Thanks, Mum, but I just want to forget the whole thing.'

'I understand.' Her mother patted her hair, and Beth closed her eyes, remembering how she used to curl up by the fire while her mother brushed and plaited her hair. She sighed. That was a long time ago.

Gail kissed Beth's cheek then hugged her. 'You'll feel better after a while. If all goes well, you'll be at university next year and there'll be lecture halls full of boys.' Beth faked a smile and felt old. She was glad she hadn't told her mother. There was no point spoiling things. There'd been enough damage done already.

Libby: 9 weeks

Tran's party was due to begin at eight but Libby asked Darren to meet her in the park at seven. He was waiting by the swings when she arrived.

'Hi,' Libby said.

'G'day,' Darren replied. They breathed dragon puffs into the misty air, and waited for each other to begin.

'I need to talk to you,' Libby whispered.

'That's why I'm here.'

'You know that night after Rick's party?' Darren nodded. 'When you didn't have an, umm, condom.' Darren's face changed. He watched Libby say the words and felt like he was starring in a bad movie. Everything was happening in slow motion. Nothing seemed real. He shivered. Now she was watching his mouth, waiting for him to say something. A truck rumbled by, then a dog barked. Normal things. Libby waited.

'Are you sure?' he said at last.

'What do you think? Of course I'm sure. I've done a test.' She held out the plastic tube. 'See? The double line means there's a kid in there.' Darren swallowed and sat down. 'The bench is wet,' Libby said. Darren stared at her. 'You don't seem very worried.'

The damp soaked through his jeans and Darren wondered if she meant the wet bench. But no, she was talking about the baby. His baby. Their baby. Oh, God, why was this happening?

'Give me a chance,' he said. 'You caught me by surprise. I thought you were going to dump me.'

'What?'

'Tonight.' He stood up and brushed his jeans. 'I thought you wanted to meet early so you could dump me. You've been so strange, and I've hardly seen you this week.'

'I've had other things on my mind.'

'Obviously.' They stared at each other. Darren wished he could run away. It wasn't fair. Why had he given Rick his last condom that night? And why hadn't Libby told him if it was a dangerous time of the month for her? Girls were supposed to know stuff like that.

'Damn it,' he shouted, kicking the bench. Libby turned and began running. 'Wait,' he called. 'I'm sorry. It's not your fault.' He ran after her and squeezed Libby to his chest. She crumpled against him. His body was warm and familiar. Libby closed her eyes. It was good to be hugged. She felt a rush of gratitude. Maybe things would be okay after all.

'You feel wonderful,' Libby mumbled, angry that she was crying again. She tried to sniff back the tears. 'I'm messing up your jumper,' she said, groping for a tissue. Darren held her tighter.

'I can wash it,' he said, stroking her hair. They stood swaying in the rain. 'Do your parents know?' Darren asked. Libby nodded into his chest.

'Mum does. She guessed two weeks ago. I've been vomiting every morning. She heard me.'

'What about your dad?'

'I asked Mum to wait, so I could tell you first.'

'How long have you known?'

'A few weeks. I did a test …'

'A few weeks! How come you didn't tell me earlier?'

'I don't know. I needed time to think. I guess I hoped it'd go away.'

'So what have you thought?'

'Lots of things. What to do. Whether to have it or not.'

Darren's hands combed her hair. He felt sick. They'd only done it a few times and he thought he'd been careful. 'And?' he asked, waiting for the verdict.

'I'm Catholic. What do you reckon?'

'Not all Catholics do what the Pope says.'

'No, but lots do!'

'So you're saying that because some old bloke in Rome reckons you should have it, you're just going to obey.'

'That *old bloke* is the head of our church.'

'Maybe, but he doesn't know anything about *your* life. What about your music? What about becoming a mum at seventeen? What kind of start is that for a kid?'

'Don't you think I've thought about all that? I've gone over it a million times, but I keep coming back to the same answer. Anyway, you don't have to be involved.'

Darren blushed. 'That's not what I'm saying. It's you who'd have to have it. I mean, I'd help and all …'

'Would you? I'm sure you don't want a kid.'

'Well, not really. I mean, one day, sure. But not yet. It'd mess up everything and Dad'd kill me.' Libby shivered. 'Come on, let's get out of the wind.' Darren put his jacket around her. He felt hollow inside, like he was going through the motions of someone else's life.

'Do you still want to go to the party?'

'Not really. Let's find somewhere where we can talk.'

'What about Mario's?'

Libby nodded. 'That'll do.'

'Have you *really* thought about this?' Darren asked as they splashed towards the café. 'There are other choices you know.'

'Not for Catholics.' Libby laughed bitterly. 'I *told* you I've thought about it. I think about it all the time. At school, at home, in the bath, in bed … I've hardly done anything else.' She stopped walking, turned and held his hands. 'Look, you need to understand. It's not only because of the Pope. I respect the church teachings, but it's still my decision. I just know I couldn't kill a baby.'

'It's not really a baby.'

'No, but it's a life. Don't you think I've been tempted? Remember how some of us had those virtual babies last year? It was fun for a few hours, then the bawling drove us mad. And the looks we got when we took them to the mall! Everyone thought they were real. I know what I'm in for.'

'But it's not just that. Bawling babies grow up. You'd be changing your life.'

'I know. But I'm sorry, Darren, I just can't have an abortion.'

'So what happens now?' Darren chewed his lip and stared at her belly. 'How far, umm, along are you?'

'Nine weeks. It's due at the end of January, and as for what happens next, that depends.'

'On me?'

'Mmm, I guess so. You, and other things.'

'I can't believe we're talking like this. You seem so calm.'

'I was a mess when I found out. I'm getting used to it now.'

'Does Ashleigh know?'

'Not yet. She hasn't spoken to me since that night I called Spud a Neanderthal.'

Darren laughed. 'It's all show. He only does it to impress girls.'

'It's not working.'

'It is with Ashleigh.'

They stepped into Mario's and ordered coffee. 'What do you want me to do?' Darren asked.

'That's up to you. It won't show for at least a month, so you still have some time to think.'

'You're sure there's no mistake?'

'Nup, sorry. Mum took me to the doctor's.'

'Shit!'

'Yeah, it was.'

Beth's rejection stung Darren. He enjoyed being in love and didn't want to be forced out of it. Before Beth, he'd practised singling out girls at parties. Not in a caveman way like Spud. Darren liked to think he was more subtle. His patience was occasionally rewarded with the odd grope, or kiss, and some relationships had progressed to the movies. But Beth was his first proper girlfriend and he'd found that devotion came easily to him. He liked knowing they'd be together on the weekend, being seen as an item. It was comfortable.

Darren reckoned Beth had lied about the flu delaying her period, but he couldn't be certain. She looked so pale that day, and she'd kept the money, but if she'd had an abortion why hadn't she told him? He would have gone with her. And if he was the father, didn't he have the right to know? Not that he'd have stopped her. Hell, he was so relieved he'd bought two packets of condoms and vowed never to do it without one again. Not even if the girl said he could. Imagine if she'd kept it? Imagine being trapped at seventeen!

Darren tried sending a carefully worded card but Beth scrawled *return to sender* across the envelope and posted it back. He waited for her at the school gate but she walked past him, flanked by a bodyguard of friends. He tried to ring her at home, but Beth's mother answered the phone.

'Elisabeth's studying,' Gail told him.

Darren wished Beth would at least talk to him. Besides wanting to get back together, he was worried about her. He kept ringing, but Gail kept answering. Her voice was antarctic, and after a while, not knowing how much Gail knew, Darren stopped calling. Stuff it, he thought. Why should I grovel?

Beth was glad, but also annoyed when he gave up. She knew it was irrational, but the things she'd liked most about Darren before were the very things that annoyed her now. The dimples which she'd thought were so cute had become ridiculous. His terrific smile bothered her, and she noticed that he always wanted to be the centre of attention. Knowing that she could have been tied to him for life gave her nightmares.

Luckily the school was big enough for her to avoid him. Darren soon got the message. He started ignoring her and going out with a girl in Year Eleven. A very pretty girl that everyone liked. Beth hated him even more.

**

The nurse had lied. Beth stared at her reflection. The colour had not returned to her cheeks. She felt grey. Colourless. Her skin was bad and her hair looked ratty. She wasn't eating well. Beth knew her hormones were largely to blame. The abortion must have been a shock for her body, but the change wasn't just physical.

Teachers had always described her as confident, outgoing, a natural leader, but now she couldn't be bothered with anything. She felt like a popped tyre. Getting through the day, trying to be normal, took all her energy. Even Ashleigh swallowed her pride and asked what was wrong.

'You can't mope about Darren forever,' her friends said, after she didn't turn up at Tran's party. Their remedy was to go out raging – the tried and tested formula. Beth stared at them. She couldn't explain, didn't even know how to try. The gulf was too wide. An ocean of rotting dreams. She'd stopped feeling young and they hadn't. Life was serious, bad things happened. She wished it was last year and that she'd never met Darren.

Britt was the first one to lose patience. 'You're not the only one with problems,' she said. 'Stop wallowing and get on with it.'

'Give her time,' Ashleigh said. 'It's only been a few weeks since they broke up.'

'Oh come on. It's turning into such a soap opera!'

As if Darren was all she had to think about, Beth thought.

Tran didn't say anything. Beth's moodiness had created a leadership void. Tran watched for a while, then stepped neatly into her place. 'I'm going into town on Saturday,' she announced. 'Nicola said there's a new Net café in Hay Street. Anyone else want to come?' Beth was the only one who shook her head, and Tran tried not to smile. She'd been living in Beth McCrae's shadow far too long.

Libby: 11 weeks

Gail hadn't told her husband about the baby. The moment never seemed right. Things were going so smoothly right now. The business was ahead and Jim's hours had become less crazy. She'd even been able to hand the books over to the accountant. After years of fitting study around the family's needs Gail was, at last, able to follow her own path. The permaculture course she'd completed left her in the right spot at the right time. She loved landscaping and her enthusiasm rubbed off onto her students. The last months had been satisfying. Not wildly exciting but comfortable, and for Gail, at this point in her life, that was enough. She felt that God watched over them and she was content.

But that was all about to change. It had already changed. *It* was growing bigger and now Gail had to tell Jim. She knew he'd be furious. Jim still thought of Libby as his little girl – something she hadn't been for years. Gail wondered how he'd handle the disappointment. For a moment she felt smug. He never listened when she told him Libby was growing up. Then she remembered her daughter's tears. Being right was little consolation now.

'There must be some mistake,' Jim said when Gail told him.

'There isn't,' Gail replied. 'We've been to the doctor.'

'But she's too young. Libby wouldn't do anything like that.'

'We did,' Gail reminded him. Jim turned and stared out the window.

'Will Darren do the right thing?' he asked

'What do you mean?'

'Marry her of course! What do you think?'

'I don't know if I want to marry him,' Libby said, walking in from the kitchen where she'd been listening.

'What?' her father exploded. 'What!'

'I said …'

'I heard you, Elisabeth. I just don't believe my ears.' He paused. 'Has he asked you?'

'It doesn't matter if he has or hasn't. I don't even know if I want him to.'

'That means he hasn't! Do you love him?'

'I don't know …'

'You don't know?' he yelled. 'Did you hear that, Gail? Libby doesn't know if she loves the boy she's slept with!' Jim stared at his daughter. 'If you don't know whether you love him, then why in God's name did you do it?' Libby looked at the carpet. 'Did he force you?'

'No, of course not. Darren's not like that!'

Jim snorted. 'Well then?'

'I don't know, it just sort of, happened.'

'I see,' her father sneered. 'It just … happened?'

Libby nodded miserably. Gail stared at Jim. Had he forgotten? she wondered. Their own mistake stood trembling before him, yet he was blind. She wanted to reach out and shake him but her energy had disappeared along with her hopes for her daughter.

The contempt in her father's eyes made Libby flinch, but she refused to look away.

'Well,' he sniffed at last. 'There's nothing else to say, except that I don't want anything to do with the whole disgusting business. Do you hear? Nothing!' He turned away and stormed into the garden. Libby glanced at her mother, but there was no sympathy there.

'He's disappointed. You'd best keep out of his way,' Gail muttered.

Libby stared out the window, past her father, who was ripping up weeds, towards the street. Tears filled her eyes. She'd always been her father's princess. His little girl. And now he thought she was a slut. The tears rolled down her cheeks. She licked them away, taking comfort in their salty taste. How could one mistake ruin everything?

Libby stroked her flat tummy. It was hard to believe there was something growing in there. She picked up her cello, played a few notes and sighed. Frau Schmidt would have a hissy fit if she didn't practise before her lesson. But it was no use, she couldn't play. And what difference did it make now? Libby flopped onto the couch, stared at the television, and felt sorry for herself.

**

James knew something was wrong before anyone bothered to tell him. The golden girl had lost her sparkle, and all of a sudden, his dad was paying attention to him, asking him about his day at school and how the footy team was going. James wondered how long it would last. Whenever Libby and his dad had tiffs this happened. Although it hurt, James had accepted the situation years ago. It wasn't as if his dad didn't love him. James knew that he did. It was just that he adored Libby. When he heard Libby was preggers, James was rapt. This was one tiff that wasn't about to end.

'Dad, the new coach is really hopeless,' James said, choosing his moment carefully. 'The guys were wondering if you could come down and help. You know, like you did last season.'

Jim smiled. 'Now that the apprentice has settled in, I s'pose I could spare a few hours. Won't the coach mind though?'

'Nup, I reckon he's desperate!'

Jim ruffled his son's hair. 'Well we can't have the Stingrays losing all season,' he said. 'Okay, tell the boys I'll be down at the oval by five.'

'Wicked.' James did a victory lap around the kitchen and wondered whether enjoying Libby's fall from grace was something he needed to admit at confession.

**

Libby thought her father would thaw, but he didn't. When he needed to talk to her he was polite, but frosty, otherwise he avoided her and spent any spare time with James. Libby tried to start conversations with him but he grunted clipped replies. One afternoon, she cornered him while he was reading the paper. 'I know you're disappointed, Dad, but ...'

'You're right I am disappointed, now please, I don't want to talk about it. It hurts too much.'

Libby slunk into the kitchen. 'Pregnancy is supposed to be a peaceful time,' she complained to her mother who was writing permaculture notes for her class. 'This cold war atmosphere isn't good for the baby.'

'Well stop provoking him then!'

'What do you mean *provoking*? Just being in the same room gets him going. He looks at me as if I'm a whore, and won't listen when I try to tell him it only happened a couple of times.'

'I don't want to hear the details, Elisabeth, and nor does your father. What's done is done. But now that you're here, please sit down, we need to talk. I rang the adoption agency yesterday. They're going to send an information package. After we've read it we can make an appointment. They want to meet you and ...'

'What?'

Gail sighed. 'The adoption agency ...'

'Who said anything about giving the baby up for adoption?'

'Well, I just assumed ... Surely you're not thinking of keeping it? A baby would ruin all your plans. You'd regret it later!'

'How do you know?'

'I just do, Libby.'

'I don't know. It's hard to imagine a baby growing inside me. I feel sick, not pregnant.'

'Well you'd better start imagining it soon,' Gail snapped. 'There's a lot to organise. You'll need maternity clothes, iron tablets, check-ups, supportive bras. Are you going to tell your friends? And what about Darren's family? Do his parents know yet?'

Libby swallowed. 'I don't think so,' she muttered. 'His dad's speaking at a conference in Sydney. He gets home on Saturday.'

'Well, this'll be an interesting homecoming present!'

Libby jumped up and water from her glass sploshed across her mother's papers. 'Why do you always have to be so sarcastic? Getting pregnant was an accident!'

Gail looked at her ruined permaculture notes. She felt like slapping Libby, but she took a deep breath instead. 'Okay, I'm sorry. But surely you can see that you need to make some decisions ...'

'Fine, but what's that got to do with Darren's parents?'

'Okay, let's leave them out of it. What are Darren's plans?' Gail hated herself for being so cold, but the numbness inside frosted her words. 'Have you spoken about it yet?'

'About what?' Libby hissed.

'You know very well about what. Is he going to marry you?'

'They're not Catholic, Mum. He might have other ideas.'

'Is that what Darren's suggesting?'

'I told you, we haven't really spoken about it.'

'Well for goodness sakes, it's about time you did!' Gail yelled. 'This is not something that's going to disappear.' Libby glared at her mother as Jim stormed into the room.

'What the hell's going on in here?' he demanded. 'What are you doing now?'

'Why don't you ask her,' Libby cried, 'instead of always blaming me?'

Jim's eyes flicked over his daughter's belly. 'Why do you think?'

'All right, let's leave it, Jim.' Gail was shaking. 'Please.'

'Now look what you've done,' Libby's father said, putting an arm around his wife's shoulders, 'upsetting your mother again.'

'Fine, then I'll leave and stop upsetting her! I've been looking at ads in the paper anyway.'

'Oh, don't start that again!' Gail sniffed taking a deep breath. 'You need to be here with us. You'd never cope on your own. You can't even steam carrots.'

'Well if I'm hungry enough I'm sure I'll learn.'

'I suppose Darren is behind this?'

'Mum, I told you I can do this on my own.'

'Oh, Libby, grow up! You're about to become a mother. You have no idea how hard that's going to be. You'll need help ...'

'Well it's going to be a lot harder with you criticising me day and night. And Dad constantly harping on about what a disappointment I am.'

'That's not fair, he's never said ...'

'He doesn't have to. The look on his face is enough to sour my milk!'

'There's no need to be crude.'

'Well look at him! How do you think I feel having him glare at me every evening. Okay, I made a mistake, but I'm trying to make the best of it ...'

'You make it sound like bad weather at a picnic.'

'For Christ's sake. Can't you listen to what I'm saying? If I've ruined your lives, I'm sorry, but how long do I have to do penance?'

'Only the priest can give penance, so there's no need to blaspheme, and it's not our lives that you've ruined ...'

'Why don't you just say straight out what you think? That I've ruined my life.'

'All right,' Gail screamed. 'You've ruined your life! After all our love and care ...' She ran into the bedroom. Libby stared at the closed door. She'd never heard her mother cry before.

'Well, I hope you're happy now,' Jim snapped as he followed his wife into the bedroom.

It took ten minutes to pack. Libby grabbed her rucksack and walked towards The Boulevard. She rang her cousin from a phone box while she waited for the bus.

'Hi, Sally? I'm so glad you're home! It's Libby. Things aren't working out here. Do you think I could stay at your place tonight? Thanks. Yeah, I'll explain when I get there.'

Sally's flat was tiny. She shared with Ruby who was also doing economics at uni. Libby dumped her pack and told them about the latest argument. Sally rang Gail to let her know where Libby was, then she ordered some takeaway.

'What did Mum say?' Libby asked while they waited for the pizza to be delivered.

'Not much, but she sounded like my mum when she's furious — civilised, but you know she's fuming underneath! It must run in the family.' Sally smiled. 'Are you okay though? Nothing's wrong with the baby?' Ruby stood up to clear away the plates.

'No, the baby's okay. But after today, I'm not sure what to do.'

'What do you mean?'

'Mum reckons I should have it adopted.'

'Is that what you want?'

Libby picked at the edges of the pizza box. 'I don't know,' she answered. 'After the initial shock, everything seemed fated. I was sitting by the beach, trying to imagine being a mother, and I knew I had to keep it. The thought was scary, but clear. I didn't even think about adoption until Mum started rabbiting on about it. She said a childless couple could give the baby so much more. The way she sees it, there's no other choice! And I can't even mention the word 'baby' to Dad. As far as he's concerned, Snow White is up the duff!'

Sally smiled and took a tub of ice-cream from the freezer. 'But are you sure you want to keep it? What about studying music next year? Wouldn't you regret giving that up?'

'I don't know. Maybe I could study part-time or defer for a year. When I decided to have the baby, I never worried about where we'd live, or how I'd find the money to feed us. I even thought Mum might help. Talk about stupid, hey?'

'I guess it's a shock for her.'

'She's not the only one!'

'What about Darren?'

'What about him?' Libby was wary.

'Does he want you to keep it?'

'He says it's up to me. We haven't made any commitments. I think he's still hoping the problem will disappear.'

'That's not likely. Unless you have an abortion.' Libby shook her head.

'Have you been to Centrelink yet?' Sally asked.

'No, I keep putting it off.'

'Why?'

'I don't know.' Libby twisted her hair checking for split ends. 'I don't want them guessing my age and making judgements.'

'I'm sure they're not like that. You won't be the first young mum they've seen. They probably get all sorts.'

'Thanks!'

'You know what I mean! But you should go down and register. It's not the dark ages. Single mothers are entitled to support.'

'Yeah, but how much?'

'I don't know. It must be enough to live on. And if you get a pension you wouldn't have to stay at home.'

'Well that'd solve one problem.'

'There's an office near the bank. While you're at it, there's a women's centre in Subiaco. They should have any information you need.'

'I guess you're right. Mum reckons I need to make plans before I get much bigger.'

'You may as well find out what's available.'

'Yeah, you're right. Umm, Sally, I really appreciate being able to come over. Do you reckon I could stay here for a few days? I promise I'll be gone by the weekend.'

'It's cool with me, but you'll have to check with Ruby.'

'It's fine with me too,' Ruby called from her room. 'Sorry to eavesdrop, but it's a small flat.'

'Thanks, Ruby,' Libby answered. 'I just need time to sort out what to do. I can't think at home.'

**

Libby woke early to vomit, then went back to doze on Sally's fold-out couch. She pulled open the blinds and watched silver-eyes darting into the bushes outside the flats. Libby liked this time of the morning, lying in bed listening to birds squawk as she planned the day.

She leant against the cushions and put her hands over her unborn child, wondering how long until she'd feel the first kicks. Then she remembered her mum's words. *You'd regret it later.* Would she? Or was her mum wrong? She knew she'd regret not knowing what her kid was like. But was it fair to bring up a child alone?

Then again, what would happen if its adopted parents split up? It could still end up with one parent. Or they might both die. Would it then become a ward of the state? Libby folded her hands over her navel and pressed. Her skin sprang back like a prize-winning sponge. It was weird. Everything had changed and yet there was no visible difference. She sighed. It was a pity Ashleigh was snubbing her. She would have loved to ask her advice.

Libby folded the bed back into a sofa and went to have a shower. She shouldn't have called Spud a Neanderthal, but sometimes it was hard to keep quiet. She hated the way he put on that macho act, especially when he treated her best friend like a hunting trophy.

The hot water felt wonderful. Libby tried to relax and stop worrying. When she came out, Sally was rushing about in her dressing-gown. 'Muesli?' she asked. 'Or toast?'

'Just tea, thanks.'

'You'll need more than tea to feed a baby,' Sally said.

'Tell that to my stomach. I can't keep anything down till mid-morning.'

'You sure?' Sally was smothering her toast in peanut butter.

'Mmhmm, just tea. But if you have a phone book, I'll look up the number of the women's centre.'

'Yeah, good idea. The directory's in the kitchen drawer. Third one down.'

**

47

The Centrelink office opened at nine. Libby was early, so she rested in a bus shelter and watched commuters rush to beat the red traffic light. Watching them was relaxing. It took her mind off her queasy tummy.

By five to nine a queue was forming. Libby stood up and joined the line. The doors opened and she trotted after the others towards a machine that spat out numbers. She wasn't sure which button to choose, so she pressed the one for general inquiries. A TV was mounted on the wall. Libby watched Big Bird sing a sharing song with Oscar while she waited for her number to appear on the screen.

The woman behind the counter was friendly. 'How can I help you?' she asked.

'I was umm ... wondering if you've got any information about pensions and things like that for single mothers.'

'There's a pile of brochures on that table and I can give you an application form. Was the information for yourself?'

The question caught Libby by surprise. 'Umm, yes, I guess so.'

'Okay,' the woman smiled. 'Why don't you take some pamphlets to read. It doesn't look like baby's due for a while yet.' She paused. 'Will your parents or partner be supporting you at all?'

'I'm not really sure yet.'

The woman hesitated, but she kept smiling. 'Well after you've read the pamphlets, come back, and I can answer your questions. My name's Vivian.' She held out her card, waited for Libby to stand then buzzed her next client.

Libby sat in a café opposite the Centrelink office and

read about assets and pensions. The bloke at the next table smiled as she ordered, but Libby ignored him. In a few months he wouldn't want to know her. She sipped her coffee and tried to convince herself that this was really happening. When her second cup was empty, she walked back to Sally's flat, collected her rucksack, and left a note.

> *Thanks for the space to think. I know that it's*
> *right for me to keep this baby, and it seems that*
> *I can get a pension. Mum and Dad will freak,*
> *but it's my body, so it has to be my decision.*
> *I've gone home to tell them. I may as well get it*
> *over with. Wish me luck. I'll let you know how*
> *it goes.*
>   *Thanks heaps, Libby xx*

**

Libby's parents were in the kitchen.

'Well, look who's decided to return,' her father said. 'I hope you've had a good, hard think about your behaviour.'

'Jim ...' Gail began, but Libby interrupted.

'I went to Centrelink this morning,' she announced.

'Centrelink? What for?'

'After the baby's born, I'll be eligible for a Sole Parent Allowance.'

'But you won't need that, Libby. Once the baby's adopted, you can go back to school. Put things back the way they were. You can redo Year Twelve, then go to uni just as you planned.'

'Mum, nothing will ever be the way it was. And

there's no way I'm going back to school. Ever. I'd rather die!'

'But, Libby, you're being silly. I thought we'd decided ...'

'No, *you* decided!' Libby yelled. 'You've never asked what *I* think I should do.'

'Darling,' Gail said quietly. 'You think you know what you want, but believe me, keeping this baby would be a mistake.'

'How do you know?'

'I just do.' She flicked her hand at a fly and Libby flinched. It was as if she was the insect.

'If I find a cheap flat, with a Sole Parent Allowance and Rent Assistance, the baby and I could manage. Other people do.'

'And what about Darren?' her father asked.

Libby blushed. 'I don't know, we haven't decided anything yet.'

Darren's new girlfriend was called Sasha. Beth watched them eat lunch together and wondered whether they were whispering the same words and doing the same things she'd done with Darren. Sasha was younger than Darren. She was petite with long hair and dinky freckles sprinkled across her nose. Britt reckoned she modelled on weekends for her family's fashion house. A perfect size ten.

They looked great together. Darren's Viking bones made Sasha seem tiny and they were both blonde with toothpaste smiles. Their happiness was a magnet. Beth wondered if she'd gazed at Darren with kitten eyes the way Sasha did. She wanted to ask her girlfriends but she was too embarrassed, and lately she'd become vague. Beth knew they were fed up with her and she didn't blame them.

During the holidays, when she wasn't studying or torturing her cello, Beth lay on her bed listening to CDs. One day her ex-best friend, Ashleigh, came over to find out why Beth hadn't returned her calls.

'Hi,' she called to Gail who was reclaiming the last patches of front lawn.

'Hello, how do you think these will look?' Gail pushed back her hair and nodded to a forest of seedlings.

'Good,' Ashleigh replied. Anything green thrived when Gail touched it. Over the past few years, she'd turned a bare yard into a bushy, suburban hideaway.

'Is Beth in?'

'Mmm, she's in her bedroom, studying perhaps. Go on in.' Ashleigh banged on her friend's door.

'What d'you want?' Beth yelled, expecting her brother. Ashleigh opened the door.

'Are you going to tell me what's wrong?' she asked.

Beth sat up in surprise. 'How did you get in?'

'Your mum told me to come up. Now, are you going to tell me?'

'What do you mean?'

'What's wrong? You've been so strange lately and you didn't put your name down for a ticket to the fundraising concert.'

'I've been strange! You're the one who stopped talking to me.'

'But then I bit my tongue and tried to make up. Remember?'

'You've still been frosty.'

'Well, what did you expect?'

'Okay, I'm sorry. I shouldn't have called him a Neanderthal, but Ash, you know, sometimes ...'

'Don't start, Beth. I like him, okay? That macho stuff is all on the surface. He only does it in front of people. When we're alone, he's really sweet.'

'But, Ashleigh ...' Beth looked at her friend's face and decided it was time to shut up. 'You're right, I should butt out. I'm sure I'll discover the real Spud once I know him better ...'

Ashleigh beamed. 'I knew you'd come round eventually. So can we have a truce? I've missed you. It's not the same with Britt and Tran.'

Beth hugged her. 'I know. I'm sorry I've been a pain.'

'How come you haven't bought a ticket to the concert?'

'I've been studying,' Beth said.

'We're all studying. That doesn't mean you can ignore what's happening to our forests.'

'Ashleigh, please. Don't start lecturing me. I don't feel like dancing.'

'Then just go along and listen to the music.'

'Yeah sure. And how stupid would that look.'

'Who cares? Anyway, no one would notice. You've been acting weird since you dropped Darren ... or since he dropped you.'

'I dropped him!'

'Whatever. I've been waiting for you to tell me about it.'

'There's nothing to tell.'

'C'mon, Beth. I thought we were friends.'

'I don't want Britt and Tran to know.'

'Thanks a lot. Since when have I blabbed secrets?'

'Sorry. It's just hard to know where to start.'

'You could begin with Darren. One minute you were raving on about how hot he is, then you wouldn't speak to him, then after we helped scare him off, you spent last week drooling over him and Sasha.'

'I did not!'

'Well that's what everyone at school thinks.' Ashleigh kicked off her shoes and curled up on the end of Beth's bed. 'What did he do that was so dreadful?'

'He got me pregnant.'

'What!' Ashleigh checked Beth's tummy, then looked quickly away.

'It's okay. It's gone. I had an abortion.'

Ashleigh stared. 'When? Why didn't you tell me?'

Beth shook her head. 'I went in last month. It was horrible. I wanted to tell you, but we weren't speaking.'

'Did Darren go with you?'

Beth snorted. 'I didn't ask him.'

'You should have told me. I would have come.'

'I know …'

'I can't believe you didn't tell me!'

Beth sighed. Ashleigh looked so disappointed. 'If it's any consolation, I regretted not having you there. I had to run past all these fanatics. Then on the way home, the driver kept staring at me. I really wished you were with me.'

Ashleigh brightened a little. 'What did your mum say?'

'She doesn't know.'

Ashleigh chewed a nail. 'Your dad?'

'Get real!'

'How about Darren?'

'I don't know. I told him my period was late because of the flu and that everything's okay. Then I just stopped seeing him and wouldn't answer his calls. He must have guessed.'

'Where did you go, you know … to have it done?'

'There's a clinic in town.'

'What about paying for it?'

'I used Sally's Medicare card, and Darren left some money in my school bag. That helped.'

'How come you dumped him then?'

'I don't know. He got off so easily, while I got all the pain and guilt. I can't stop feeling angry with him.'

'But if he didn't know …'

'He must have guessed! Otherwise why would he leave the money?'

'What else did you want him to do?'

'I don't know.' Beth sighed. 'It sounds crazy, but I wanted him to support whatever decision I made.'

'Maybe he would have.'

'Maybe, but we'll never know now.'

'What about church? Have you been to confession?'

Beth looked away.

'If it helps,' Ashleigh continued, 'Mum's got a book that reckons church opposition to abortion is based on a male agenda to keep women serving their children and husbands. I could lend it to you.'

'Ashleigh ...' Beth warned.

'It says that letting women choose would be dangerous, a bit like rocking a boat, a huge, old, leaky boat.'

'Ashleigh, I don't want to talk about it, okay? I don't know what I'll do about church, but the rest of it is over, like Darren and me. I just want to forget about it.'

'Okay. Is there anything I can do?'

Beth grinned. 'Yeah, stop lecturing me about the church and going to your concert.'

Libby: 13 weeks

Libby and her mother went into town to shop for a bra with 'good support'. The assistant in the lingerie department at Myers smirked knowingly as they walked towards the maternity section but Gail surprised her. 'We'd like a maternity bra for my daughter,' she said in a bossy voice. 'She's thirteen weeks pregnant.'

The two women were like a pair of dogs sorting out dominance. Once the pack order was established, operations ran smoothly. While Libby blushed, the assistant backed down. The change was subtle but enough for Libby to be grateful that her mother was with her.

'Isn't there anything less like an armoured tank?' Libby asked, as the assistant handed her a dangerous looking selection. The older women closed ranks. 'If you don't wear a sturdy bra during pregnancy, your breasts will end up looking like something a tank has squashed,' her mother said.

'Support in these early weeks is so important,' the assistant droned. Gail nodded and said they'd take two.

'But does it have to be so big?' Libby complained. 'Aren't there any with lace or anything?'

The assistant glared at her. 'Maternity bras are

designed for support, not looks,' she said as she zapped the bar code and bent to wrap the arsenal. At the counter Libby noticed a black version in the box.

'Let's at least get one in black,' she said. Gail hesitated, then asked the assistant to swap one white bra for the black version.

They left the lingerie section and while Gail dithered in the make-up department Libby tried on straw hats and thought about Darren. He'd told her that he needed space to think, so they'd decided to have a break from each other. That was fine, until Libby overheard Ashleigh telling Britt she'd seen Sasha, a Year Eleven girl, hanging around him.

Libby had swallowed her pride and gone over to Ashleigh's house. After the first frosty moment, Libby'd apologised for calling Spud a Neanderthal and asked Ashleigh to tell her the gossip about Darren and Sasha. Then she'd told Ashleigh that she was thirteen weeks pregnant.

'What do you think about this colour? Is it too bright?' Libby stopped daydreaming and turned to look at the lipstick her mum was rubbing on her wrist.

'No, it's fine.'

'Or do you think this is better?'

Who cares, Libby felt like screaming. 'I like the first one,' she said.

'Me too,' her mum agreed. She paid the heavily painted assistant, then asked Libby what she wanted for lunch.

'You choose,' Libby replied. Their favourite sushi bar was nearby, but after seeing how little change her mum received at the bra counter, Libby didn't want to push her luck.

'Is your tummy okay?' Libby nodded.

'Good, how about we go and have sushi?' Libby smiled. She knew her mum was trying hard to be positive.

'What about that listeriosis thing? Can I eat raw fish at the moment?'

'I'm not sure. You could order Californian roll without the prawn.'

'Okay.' Libby wanted to link arms with her mum but something stopped her. Although they'd called a truce, Libby wasn't sure that the battle was over.

Beth: 14 weeks

Beth flung off her doona and stared at Marina's pale face. 'Stop it!' the girl yelled.

'It's okay.' Beth reached out to comfort the shape hovering above her bed.

'No!' The girl's face was contorted with rage. 'No it's not okay!' She glared at Beth then began fading.

'Wait,' Beth whispered. 'What can I do?'

'Stop it,' the girl said. 'Just stop it.'

'But how?'

The face dissolved until only the world-weary eyes remained. 'It's not okay.' They blinked. 'Not okay. Just stop it. Stop him. Please stop it.'

Beth flicked on her bedside light. Marina's face had seemed so real. But where was she now? What was happening to her? Beth shivered. The memory of them sitting together in the waiting room was so clear. Except that it was as if she was looking down on the scene. As if she was a little soul looking down …

Beth pulled up her doona and switched off the lamp. She lay in the dark longing for someone to hold her and say that what she'd done was okay. Then she folded her hands over her flat tummy and began to cry.

Libby: 15 weeks

The morning sickness had gone, but now Libby was constantly hungry. She tried not to pigout at school, but every morning around ten o'clock she had an overwhelming urge to scoff iced donuts. As soon as the siren rang, Libby raced to the canteen.

'I thought you were trying to diet,' Tran said, sipping iced coffee.

'That was last month,' Libby muttered between bites. 'This month I'm enjoying myself.' Tran raised her eyebrows and went to chat with Britt. Libby saw them watching her. 'Do you think they've guessed?' Libby asked Ashleigh.

'I don't know, but I need to show you something after school.'

'What?'

'I'll tell you later. I have to whiz home and collect it. Can you meet me at the park at four o'clock?'

'What about a hint?' Ashleigh shook her head.

'Okay,' Libby said, licking icing off her fingers, 'I'll see you at four.'

**

Libby balanced on a swing and watched a group of kids digging in the sandpit. Then she saw Ashleigh cycling along the footpath. 'Well?' Libby asked.

Ashleigh leant the bike against the fence and pulled a paper bag out of one pannier. 'A present,' she said holding it out. 'And I hope you appreciate it! You should have seen the look I got buying it in my school uniform.'

'What is it?' Libby asked.

'Open it and see.'

Libby opened the paper bag. It was a book: *Waiting for Baby – all you need to know*, she read, flipping the pages. 'Cool, look at the pictures.'

'Yeah, that's what I liked. And at the back it tells you week by week what's happening inside the oven. What week are you now? Fourteen?'

'Fifteen.'

'Look it up and see what it says.'

'*Your heart has enlarged and is pumping 20 per cent more blood. Baby's hair is becoming thicker on both the head and brows. Your clothes are probably becoming tighter.*' Libby pulled a face and held up her jumper to show the safety pins holding her shirt together. 'They're right about that,' she sighed.

'Some girls would kill for boobs like that.'

'Talk to one of the boys. I'm sure they'd oblige.'

'Forget it,' Ashleigh replied. 'Lift-up bras are a lot less trouble. What else do they say? Read out last week's.'

'*Week Fourteen,*' Libby began. '*Your uterus will have stretched to the size of a large grapefruit and the linea nigra has probably appeared.*'

'The linea what?'

'*This is a dark line of skin,*' Libby read, '*which runs down the centre of the abdomen over the rectus muscle.*'

'Ew, it sounds painful.'

'No, it's just a shadow, but I was wondering what it was.' She smiled. 'Thanks Ash, this is a great present.'

'Can I see it?'

'See what?'

'The line, of course.'

'It's a bit gross ...'

Libby lifted the edge of her uniform and pointed to the line creeping out of her undies and across her belly. Ashleigh stared.

'It's amazing to think there's a baby in there. Can you feel it yet?'

'No, I just feel sick and bloated. But look, the book goes on to say that the line fades after giving birth. That's a relief. I thought I'd be stuck with a stripe.'

Ashleigh dug her foot into the sand. 'Libby, there's something else I should tell you.'

'Mmm,' Libby said flicking the pages.

'Tran was asking about you. She umm ... I think she's guessed.'

Libby closed the book. 'What did she say?'

'Nothing specific. Just general things.'

'Like what?'

'Well, she was asking how come you and Darren broke up.'

'What did you say?'

'You know, what you told me. That he was immature and full of himself.'

'And ...'

'She said you were crazy. That he was really hot. Then she wanted to know if I thought you'd changed. I asked in what way and she gave me this strange look.'

'When was this?'

'After recess.'

'What about Britt?'

'If Tran knows, she will too.'

'Damn! That's all I need.'

'Why don't you just tell them? They're your friends and they're going to find out soon anyway.'

'Yeah, but not yet. I need more time.'

'What for?'

'I don't know. I'm just not ready.'

'Have you decided when you're going to leave?'

'What, school?'

'Mmm.'

'No, not yet. I really want to finish Year Twelve, even if I have to do half of it from home. Did I tell you that Mum rang the Education Department? They said I could stay at school as long as I wanted. If I do all the assignments, I can even sit the exams.'

'That's good.'

'Yeah, I was surprised. It seems I'm not the only one. They kept talking about the policy for *girls in my situation.*'

'You see, it's not so strange.'

'But I'm the only one at our school.'

'That you know about …'

Libby laughed. 'Have you got a secret?'

'Maybe!'

'About staying at school, I'm going to try and stay for most of this term.'

'You won't be able to keep your jumper on till October.'

'I know. I was boiling last week.'

'That's probably when Tran guessed.'

'How do you mean?'

63

'Don't you remember? On that really warm day. Wednesday wasn't it? We were sitting down the back. Everyone had their jumper off except you, and Britt kept asking why you weren't hot.'

'That's right.'

'And she was grinning at Tran.'

'Well, if they've guessed, who else knows?'

'Maybe just them. Still, I reckon you should tell them, before it, umm, gets round.' Libby glared at her. 'Sorry,' Ashleigh said, 'but people aren't stupid.'

'I am,' Libby muttered. Ashleigh looked away and wondered what to say.

Beth: 16 weeks

Beth threw herself into her studies. She'd lost ground during the weeks of wallowing, but third term was revision so at least she hadn't missed anything new.

'Only eight weeks until the mock exams,' their maths teacher told the class. As if they needed reminding. The exams loomed over everything. Their lives were divided into before and after the exams. Everyone talked about what they'd do as soon as their last exam was over. But they didn't spend all their time studying. Playing cello helped Beth relax, Britt watched old movies and Tran was into surfing. When she wasn't studying, Ashleigh was organising her *Save the Forests* concert. The money raised was going towards a media blitz in the weekend papers, trying to show people the truth about logging old growth forests.

'How come you're not going to the concert?' Britt asked Beth.

'She's probably far too busy studying,' Tran muttered.

'Of course I'll be going,' Beth snapped.

'But you said ...'

'I changed my mind.'

'That's great,' Ashleigh said, hugging her friend. 'It's only a few weeks away now and we need all the support we can get.'

'Are people dressing up, or is it just jeans and T-shirts?'

'Whatever. Rick reckons he and Spud are coming as numbats.'

'Spud dressed as a numbat! That's something I have to see. Are you sure he's not coming as a chainsaw?'

'They said numbats, but who knows with those two?'

'Well, my green Docs should fit the mood, and maybe a rainbow T-shirt, with a floaty skirt and Save The Whales badge.'

'It's a serious cause, Beth.'

'I know. It was a joke! You keep telling me to lighten up. Besides, I don't have any floaty skirts.'

**

Gail was trying not to nag. 'You don't need to do that,' she said when she caught Beth scrubbing the shower. 'It's sweet and I appreciate it, but why don't you leave it until after the exams?' Beth took a deep breath and ignored the pains in her belly. She had to keep busy. The bleeding had begun just after breakfast. It was her first period since the abortion and it was making her remember things she wanted to forget.

'It's relaxing,' Beth argued. 'It makes me feel better.'

'Go for a walk,' Gail replied. 'Get some fresh air. You look pale.'

So Beth cleaned her room when no one was looking and wondered if compulsive cleaning was some kind of penance. Lately, a burning need to organise her books and papers surprised her at odd moments, and she'd become paranoid about dust.

Beth hadn't been to confession in weeks. There seemed no point mentioning petty issues if she was going to hide such a big one. No amount of prostration and Hail Marys could equal a child, bring it back to life. But given the choice, Beth knew she'd do the same again. So what was the point in asking forgiveness? Wouldn't that be hypocritical?

It wasn't something she could discuss with their priest. Father Patrick had known her since she was a girl. Of course he would honour the sanctity of the confessional and not tell her parents but Beth wondered if she could bear his disappointment. He'd given her her first Holy Communion and was a close family friend. The idea of disillusioning him was as painful as the thought of her parents knowing. Luckily, studying was a convenient excuse for not going to church.

'I really need to summarise these last few chapters,' Beth said the first week she missed mass. The following week she was halfway through a maths paper when Gail came to see if she was ready. 'I'll go during the week,' she muttered. Gail raised her eyebrows but said nothing. Although Beth was relieved, she missed the Sunday service. She especially missed the hymns. Beth loved filling her lungs to sing the songs of praise that thousands of worshippers before her had sung. Sometimes she could almost feel the souls of the faithful shining through the stained glass to join the chorus.

Beth sighed. Church provided a fellowship that was hard to explain. She reached for her cello and plucked a string. Maybe she could work out the notes of her favourite hymns.

Libby: 17 weeks

Libby went to her second antenatal visit alone. She liked Dr Wong and felt more relaxed this time knowing that her mother wasn't sitting tight-lipped in the waiting room.

'Have you felt any movements?' the doctor asked.

'No, I don't think so.'

'It's a bit early yet, but it shouldn't be long. At first it's soft, like a butterfly's wing brushing inside you.'

'It sounds nice,' Libby said shyly.

'It is.' Dr Wong smiled and took her blood pressure. 'How are things at home?' she asked.

Libby hesitated. 'Not too bad,' she said. 'I'm moving into a flat of my own soon.'

'Are your parents happy about that?'

'They'll be glad to get rid of me.'

'What about your boyfriend?'

'We're not sure. He might move in when he finishes school.' *If* we're back together, she thought.

'Sounds like you've got it all organised.'

Libby nodded and wondered why kind Dr Wong made her feel like a child.

**

Darren asked if they could meet at *Mario's*. Libby

walked in after school and saw him sitting at a booth. He looked like a cornered rabbit. 'Want a coffee?' She nodded, and as he ordered a cappuccino for her, she wondered what he'd decided.

'How's it going?' Darren asked.

'Not bad.' It was hard to stop herself asking about the Year Eleven girl.

'I told Dad.'

'What'd he say?'

'Lots of stuff. You don't want to know the details.' I do, Libby thought, but she didn't interrupt him. 'Once he stopped ranting, he offered to help. If we want to rent a unit, he'll pay the bond. There are a few places near the uni. I'm going to look at one later.'

'Really? Is that what you want?' He nodded, but Libby suspected that if a way out presented itself, he'd bolt. 'You don't have to, Darren. I can do this on my own.'

'That's not fair, Libby, and besides, I want to. It's my kid too.' He reached out and squeezed her hand. 'At least we can try.'

Libby tried to smile, but ended up sniffling again. 'Sorry,' she laughed. 'It's my hormones.'

**

As she walked home, Libby wondered what to tell her mother. If there was any chance of her and Darren making a go of it, Libby knew she'd have to move out. They needed space and a place of their own. She couldn't believe Darren's dad was going to help. From the little Darren had said, she knew Mr Erikson blamed her for *trapping* his son. Her own parents weren't any better. At least Mr Erikson was prepared to help out financially.

Gail was in the kitchen shredding newspaper for the worm bin. Libby sat beside her, wondering how to begin. 'If we move into a place of our own, we might be happy. Darren's parents have offered to pay the bond,' she said, ripping up the business pages and reaching for the arts supplement.

'So he's told them at last.'

Libby nodded.

'What else did they say?'

'Darren just said that they were disappointed, but they'd pay any costs.'

Gail sniffed and ripped faster.

'That won't be necessary,' Jim shouted from the lounge room. 'You can tell Dr Big-Shot-Dentist-Erikson that his son's done enough. We don't want his charity! If you need any extras we can pay for them.' Libby and her mum exchanged glances.

'Thanks, Dad,' Libby mumbled.

He grunted. 'It's only until January. If you still don't want to give up the child, you can pay your way once the pension cheques start arriving.'

Libby flinched. 'Of course,' she muttered sarcastically, but he was too far away to hear.

**

'Only a few more weeks of school,' Libby whispered as Ashleigh dropped her lunch wrapper into a bin.

'You've decided to leave?'

'I had coffee with Darren yesterday. We're back together and he's looking at flats near the uni. Once I've decided on one, his dad will sign the lease and I can move out. '

'Excellent! What about Darren?'

'He'll move in later.'

'Are you sure?'

'What do mean?'

'You know, to be back with Darren.'

Libby nodded. 'Mmm, it feels like the best way.'

'When will you leave school?'

'After I move. That saves me working out the bus timetable. Besides, it's getting obvious now. I don't think Britt and Tran are the only ones who've guessed.'

Ashleigh nodded. 'Last week Nicola asked me why you weren't doing Phys Ed any more.'

'What did you say?'

'That you had a virus. I muttered something about chronic fatigue, but she didn't look convinced.'

'Thanks for trying,' Libby said.

'Will you tell the others before you go?'

'Only Britt and Tran. Mum and Dad are going out next Saturday. They said I can ask you all over to watch a video. I'll tell them then.'

'At last. It's been hell trying to keep it a secret. Specially when they keep hinting.' She paused. 'How are you feeling? Has the morning sickness stopped?'

Libby nodded. 'Thank God.'

'So what are the latest developments?'

'Well, the book reckons the baby has finger and toenails now.'

'They'll come in handy.'

'Yep, and as for me, I'm sweating more and my nipples have darkened.'

'Cool.'

Libby laughed. 'Yeah, it'd be good if they stay this way. I like them better in brown.'

71

Beth: 18 weeks

Beth craved junk food. After school, before James got home, she'd shovel down a bag of chips or gobble half a tub of ice-cream before slinking away to the toilet to throw it up. She became sneaky, eating biscuits or cake from different packets so it wasn't obvious. Her mum's cooking chocolate disappeared; so did the after-dinner mints and corn chips.

'Everyone warned me a teenage boy would eat me out of house and home,' Gail said whenever food went missing. Beth felt repulsive, but strangely proud of her cunning. Although she'd lost weight she still felt fat. Her face was pale and her skin looked drained and blotchy, like a grimy sink. Phantom cravings ruled her life and Beth spent all her allowance on takeaways. Soon she began avoiding mirrors.

Gail dragged her off to the doctor for a check-up and Beth felt naked, sure that he could somehow tell what her body had been through. 'How are your periods?' he asked as he checked her ears. She didn't want to tell him they'd become more painful, because then he'd ask why.

'Okay,' she replied.

'No problems? They're not too heavy or irregular?'

'They're fine,' Beth answered coldly.

'Right, well she's a bit run down,' he said to Gail as if Beth wasn't there. 'And she shouldn't lose any more weight.' He checked her birth date on the file. 'Ah, she's doing her final year at school, is she?' Gail nodded. 'Well, that's probably it then,' he said closing her file. 'It happens to a lot of kids, especially girls. Make sure she gets plenty of exercise and fresh food.' Beth felt like she'd been taken to the vet. When the doctor opened the door for them to leave, she was tempted to bark in his face.

'I know it's a heavy year,' he said in a jokey voice. 'You're probably a bit of a junk food addict ...'

'Not really,' Beth interrupted, wishing their regular doctor hadn't left to specialise in obstetrics.

'Hmm, well, eat sensibly. Listen to your mum and try to relax. The exams will be over before you know it.'

'I know he's not as nice as Dr Ann,' Gail said on the way home, 'but there was no need to be rude. I knew you weren't eating enough. You're too thin. I'm worried about you.'

Beth sighed. 'I'm fine, Mum. I told you that before we went.'

'And you need to get out on weekends,' Gail continued. 'What's happened to Tran and Britt? You used to always talk about them.'

'They're studying. We're about to sit for our final exams. It's the most important year of our lives. Remember?'

'There's no need to take that tone with me. I know the exams are important, but you'd concentrate better if you took regular breaks.'

'Mum ...'

'Don't roll your eyes at me. There are other things in life besides textbooks and cello. I may be ancient, but I've done my share of studying.' Beth linked arms with her mother.

'Okay,' she said, relieved that the doctor's visit was over. 'Let's stop at the deli and get an ice-cream.'

'You know I'm watching my weight,' her mum replied.

'What a hypocrite! You need to set a good example. I'll eat if you will.'

Gail sighed. 'All right,' she agreed, 'but don't be surprised if I can't fit into my black dress for your graduation.'

Libby: 19 weeks

Britt and Tran arrived together.

'We brought a snack,' they said, dumping a cache of chips and chocolate onto the floor.

'Great.' Beth shook the chips into a bowl while her friends flopped onto the couch.

'What time are your parents coming home?' Britt asked as she munched a handful of chips.

'Not till late. I've got two videos, but I want to tell you something first.' Beth took a deep breath while her friends exchanged glances. 'I guess I should have told you ages ago. I don't know why I didn't. I feel a bit stupid 'coz you've probably guessed anyway ...'

'Why don't you just spit it out?' Tran suggested.

'Okay,' Beth said. 'I just want you to know that I'm pregnant.'

'What a surprise,' Tran said sarcastically.

'We were wondering when you were going to tell us.'

'So you did know.'

'We're your friends, Beth. Friends notice little things like that!'

'Who else knows?'

'We haven't said anything, but people are suspicious.'

'Well, you can broadcast it now. Today was my last

day. I'm moving into a flat.'

Britt and Tran stared at her. 'When?'

'Tomorrow. Mum went to the office yesterday and told them. I have to come back to school for the exams, but I can do the rest of my work at home.'

'What about assignments and all that?'

'Ashleigh's going to be my courier.' Libby smiled at her friend. 'She'll let me know what I have to do and collect my homework once or twice a week. Darren said he'd help also.'

'So he's the father?'

'Yeah, who else? I'm not that secretive!'

'I thought you'd broken up.'

'We were having a break. I didn't want Darren to feel forced.'

'So you'll have your own place,' Britt said. 'That's so cool. Hey, can we come over and visit?'

'Of course.'

'Is it big enough for parties?'

Libby hesitated. 'Maybe,' she said as she passed around the food. She didn't like being in crowds at the moment. Libby munched chips as her friends began describing horror birth stories they'd heard from their sisters and aunts and people on TV. 'Enough,' she said patting her belly. 'They reckon babies hear what goes on outside the womb. Stop giving her strange ideas.'

'*Her*,' they squealed. 'You never know, it could be a little Darren!'

'Show them the linea thing,' Ashleigh said as Libby stood up to get a video.

'The what?' Britt asked.

Libby sighed and pulled up her T-shirt.

**

The flat was minimally furnished. There was a table and chairs, a bed and cupboards, so Libby only needed a few bits and pieces. James stayed behind after their dad left. He felt sorry for his big sister and that was a new experience. After so many weeks he was surprised how hard-hearted his parents could be, especially their father. It made him nervous that one could fall from grace so easily. 'Where do you want this?' he asked, picking up a box.

'In the kitchen. It's pots and pans and things. Hey, thanks for helping.'

'That's okay.' James wanted to talk about the baby, but he didn't know how to begin. 'You'll be able to do what you want now.'

Libby laughed. 'Mmm,' she said, 'but soon I'll be too big to party.'

James laughed, not that it was funny. 'Will you be okay?' he asked. Libby gave him a hug.

'Of course,' she said. 'Once I put up some curtains and sort out my things, it'll be really cosy.'

James looked out the window as Libby arranged a space for her cello. 'You'll be able to watch the boats,' he said.

'Mmm,' Libby replied. 'And you can visit after school.'

'Would you mind?'

'Nah, someone'll have to let me know how the family's surviving without me, and Mum and Dad certainly aren't very communicative.'

James lifted another box and felt guilty that he'd been so pleased in the beginning. 'I reckon they're being mean,' he said simply.

Libby smiled but looked sad. 'Me too,' she replied.

**

Gail filled her glass and watched the evening colours soften her garden. Sitting amongst her plants, noticing which ones were thriving and which needed more compost, usually calmed her, but tonight she was too angry and sad and frustrated about Libby to be comforted. She realised it would be good for them all to have a break but, as she'd watched Jim drive Libby to the flat, Gail felt that she had somehow failed her daughter.

Seeing Libby's figure expand distressed her more than she could say. Maternity dresses looked too big for someone so young. So young and beautiful. A few months ago, her daughter's future had stretched glimmering into the future. Music and fun times at uni. Opportunities Gail herself had missed. But now the dream was shattered. Libby wouldn't be able to study music with a baby in tow. Not properly. She thought she could, but Gail knew she was wrong. You need discipline to master an instrument, not the compromise that babies demand, and Libby had already slipped behind in her cello practice.

Gail sighed and sipped her wine. She'd read about pushy parents and knew it was wrong to live through her kids, but she'd had such dreams for Libby. It was ironic really. Fate's way of paying her back. She'd become complacent, and now history was repeating itself. Libby had made the same mistake she had. She'd even made the same decision. Except that these days girls didn't need a bloke to stick by them: the supporting mother's pension had changed all that. Gail tried to guess what her life would have been like if she'd had that kind of safety net, and whether Darren would stick around the way Jim had. She sipped again and wondered what would have happened if she'd chosen differently?

'Your music has improved,' Gail said as Beth put down her bow. 'I guess it's all the practising you've been doing. Mrs Schmidt must be pleased.'

Beth smiled. 'Mmm, she complimented me last week. Although the way she praises, I almost missed it. *"Very good, Elisabeth. At last you have mastered the vibrato in that piece."'* Beth imitated her teacher's strict voice. Her mother laughed and asked what she was working on.

'It's the middle of Saint-Saëns' *The Swan*. If I can get this part right before next week Frau Schmidt thinks I should play it at the eisteddfod.'

'Will you have time to learn it properly?'

'I don't know. I'm okay with the beginning and end parts, so it's only the middle that needs work. Besides Mrs S reckons I play best when a piece is new. She says it sounds less stilted. "Frisch" she called it in German.'

'I still think you've taken on too much with this eisteddfod. You don't want to get behind with your other work …'

'You're the one who said I should have other interests.'

'I know. I just worry. You're still so pale … and thin.'

'Mum, stop nagging. It's not as if I'm anorexic or anything.'

Gail turned away. 'I didn't want to say anything, but ...'

'Mum! I'm fine. I ate heaps last night,' Beth said. And I didn't even throw up afterwards, she thought.

'I noticed. I was very relieved.'

'You worry too much. My weight is fine and playing the cello helps take my mind off ... other things.'

'All right, I'll stop fussing.'

'Good. Is it still okay if Ashleigh comes over?'

'Sure. James has gone to Troy's, so she can stay the night if she wants to.'

'Excellent. I'll stop at the video shop later.'

'Nothing too loud. I have to prepare work sheets for tomorrow's class.'

**

Beth waited until after the first video to tell Ashleigh that she wasn't going to the concert.

'But you've bought your ticket ...'

'I'm know. I want to support the campaign and everything, it's just ... I don't feel up to it. Darren will be there with Sasha. I heard them talking about it and I don't want to watch them hanging off each other. I'm sorry, but I'd just get angry and spoil it for the rest of you.'

'What will you do?'

'Stay home. Study I guess.'

'Beth, you need to get over it. You made the right decision. I'd have done the same. Anyway, what's done is done. Moping about feeling sorry for yourself isn't going to change anything.'

'I know. But I've paid for my ticket so at least I'm contributing.'

'That's not the point. We need people to turn up and *show* that they care.' She paused. 'Spud really is coming as a numbat. You said you wouldn't miss that for the world.'

'I know. Tran said she'd take a photo for me. Look, Ashleigh, I'm sorry. I promise I'll be there for the next one.'

'There might not be any forest to save next time!'

'You're being melodramatic. The forests need rational spokespeople. Look, if I promise to sell heaps of your raffle tickets, will you forgive me?'

Ashleigh rummaged in her bag. 'Okay.' She smiled and handed Beth five booklets.

Libby: 21 weeks

The flat was small but Libby didn't care. It was such a relief to be away from the sour atmosphere at home. The unit was on the second floor so there wasn't a garden, but the area was surrounded by parks. There was a playground down by the foreshore and even a network of cycle paths to push a pram on when the time came.

'What about the noise from the pub?' her mother asked.

'You know I can sleep through anything. Besides, being opposite the pub is the only reason we can afford to live this close to the uni.'

'I'd rather have you living near home,' Gail worried.

'If we're going to make a go of it, Darren needs to be within cycling distance of his classes. He can't afford a car.'

'Mmm, I suppose.' Her mother sighed and turned away.

**

Darren was staying at home until after the exams, so Libby had the flat to herself. The first week was fantastic. She studied each morning, then played her cello and embroidered ducks onto tiny socks and singlets in the afternoons. At dusk she took a cup of tea onto the balcony and sat in a crumbling cane chair which the last tenant had left.

The weather was fine. Libby went for long walks along the foreshore and tried not to worry. She watched yachties take their boats out, enjoying the first warm days of spring while the suits parked their flash cars and strolled towards a seafood lunch at the jetty restaurant. All the while she felt as if her own life was in limbo. Before the baby. Before the exams. Before Darren moved in.

Ashleigh came after school to deliver assignments and keep her up on the school news. Libby knew there was gossip about Darren and Sasha, but her friend was vague whenever she asked about it.

Ashleigh was reading aloud from the *Waiting for Baby* book when Libby felt the first prod. *'Baby is probably testing her reflexes now. She is about twenty centimetres long and is kicking and grasping.'*

'Hey, stop reading. I just felt something! Here, give me your hand. Can you feel anything?'

Ashleigh shook her head. Libby waited. 'Maybe it was my imagination.'

'Do you want me to read the rest?'

Libby nodded and stroked her belly.

'Some babies find their thumb around this time and learn to suck for comfort. This is a good time for mothers to begin a relaxation routine.'

Libby grinned. 'How can I relax when my music assignment is due?'

'How are you going with it?'

'Hopeless. You were smart choosing home science.'

**

James came to visit too. He rode his bike and, depending on headwinds, could do the trip in twenty minutes. Seventeen was his record. Libby looked forward to her brother's visits. He brought homemade snacks and news from her parents. With him as their courier, it was easy for Gail and Libby to keep in touch without meeting.

**

On Saturday Darren rang to say he was coming over. 'Dad's redoing the back fence and I need to escape,' he said. Libby hesitated. She didn't have plans and she was keen to see him but it annoyed her that he needed an excuse.

'Well?' Darren asked. 'Is that okay?'

'Of course, come on over,' Libby replied, and went to change out of her tracksuit.

When he arrived she felt nervous. Darren seemed edgy too. He usually visited in the afternoons, but this time he'd arrived with an overnight bag, which he put in her bedroom. Libby felt odd. It was as if her haven had been invaded, which was silly. He'd be around permanently soon.

They spent the day playing house. Darren was a legend in the kitchen. He made herb and tomato omelettes for lunch which were perfectly light and fluffy, but when Libby asked him to tell her his secret, he refused. Libby knew he was joking, but it still annoyed her. Probably because the cake she'd baked for afternoon tea had sunk in the middle.

After lunch Darren helped Libby with her

assignments. They studied for a few hours, then bought ice-creams from Mr Whippy on the foreshore. Darren told Libby how his dad was nagging him to apply for law. 'He reckons scientists aren't appreciated. What he really means is that they're not paid enough. I told him that money isn't everyone's top priority and we had a pretty amazing fight.'

'And then you rang me?' Darren nodded.

'So it wasn't because of the fence?'

'Not really. You don't mind do you?' Libby shook her head and wondered whether he would have called if he hadn't fought with his dad.

She learnt a lot about Darren during the weekend. Besides being kind and considerate, he was reasonably tidy. He did the dishes straight after meals, hung up his clothes and made a big show of not letting her do any heavy jobs. He even nicked some roses for her from a neighbour's garden. Libby put the roses into a jam jar and tried to squash the goblin in her head that kept asking who Darren thought put out the rubbish and carted groceries four blocks from the shopping centre when he wasn't there.

She tried to ask what his family thought about them living together but he kept changing the subject, or offering to make her some tea. Neither of them mentioned marriage and Libby still wasn't sure how she felt about a wedding. A life commitment seemed so long. What she really wanted to know was whether Darren would be around for the baby's first year.

On Sunday morning she cornered him but all Darren would say was that he'd move in after their final exams and see how it went from there. Libby nodded and stroked her belly.

When she played her cello, Beth lost the nagging feeling of guilt that was always waiting to bite. She'd spent hours preparing for the eisteddfod and knew she was playing better than ever. Frau Schmidt was jubilant. *'Wunderbar!'* she declared. 'There is a new depth in your music, Elisabeth. You see, you just needed to work more.'

But Beth knew it wasn't the extra hours of practice which had strengthened her music. It came from somewhere inside. As if by acknowledging pain she could attempt the expression of it. Frau Schmidt encouraged Beth to add a lighter piece to her performance, but after listening to her rendition of Saint Saens' *The Swan*, she shrugged and told Beth to play what she felt was best. Of all her friends and family, Beth suspected Frau Schmidt was the only one who guessed something had happened during the year. It was difficult to hide when she played.

**

Beth was fifth on the program. There were twelve entrants in her age group. The girl before her was another one of Frau Schmidt's students. Skye had been playing since she was tiny. Her piece was the minuet

Frau S had originally suggested Beth play. As Beth listened to Skye practise backstage she knew the best she could hope for was second place.

'It doesn't sound as if you need it, but good luck anyway,' she said trying to sound sincere.

Skye smiled. 'Thanks, you too,' she said, rubbing more rosin onto her bow.

Beth's dad came in for a last-minute hug. 'You look great,' he told her. 'I like your hair like that.'

Beth looked at her reflection. She'd slicked her hair and the combination of pale skin and her forest-green dress suited the dramatic mood of the piece she was playing. 'Thanks Dad,' she muttered.

'Entrants in item seven, this way please.'

'I'd better get back to my seat. Break a leg, Princess!'

Beth's belly usually tingled with butterflies before a performance, but tonight she felt calm as she walked into the spotlight. She waited for the piano introduction, then launched into her piece. Time seemed to stop as the melancholy tune drifted from her cello over the theatre. Beth could feel the hush of audience attention as she played the final notes. She'd slurred one note, but there was a chance the judge wouldn't notice. It was strange to choose this piece for an eisteddfod, but Beth knew by the applause that she'd performed well.

'Well done,' Skye whispered as they waited backstage for the other competitors to finish. An intense violinist with a mop of curly hair and pierced eyebrows was the tenth entrant. He played with such feeling that Beth was sure he'd win. The girl following him was also excellent until she dropped her bow halfway through the piece. She picked it up and played on, but the mood was broken and Beth knew the judge would have to mark her down.

'All contestants were professional in their presentation,' he began. 'You can be very proud of yourselves, but there has to be a winner so now it is my pleasure to announce the runner-up.' The audience stopped fidgeting. 'Could you please congratulate Skye Southern. Her performance showed outstanding technical and interpretive abilities.' Everyone clapped until he coughed and continued. 'And the overall winner has to be Matt Zanetti for his inspired rendition of the Paganini caprice. A masterful performance.'

The curly-haired boy had won. Beth wasn't surprised. His delivery was exceptional. She applauded and tried to smile as he walked out to collect his statue.

'I would also like to award two highly commended certificates,' the judge continued. 'As I said, the standard amongst these young musicians is excellent. The first certificate is awarded to Jasmine Chan who played Beethoven's *Moonlight Sonata* with admirable maturity. She shows great promise. Also highly commended is Elisabeth McCrae for the depth of emotion in her interpretive style. Such sensitivity is unusual to hear in a young person. Well done to all the entrants. There will be a short break before item eight.'

Frau Schmidt beamed as Beth and Skye stepped offstage. 'Well done girls,' she said, hugging them.

James came tearing round the corner. 'Woo woo,' he said. 'My sister's famous.'

'Dag!' she told him, trying not to smile. 'It's only a highly commended.'

'Still …'

'Good on you, Princess,' Jim said while Beth's mum hugged her.

'Only a highly commended,' she repeated, trying to keep things in perspective.

'Such sensitivity,' James droned, 'from someone with a depth of emotion …'

'Let's go to Mario's for coffee and cake to celebrate,' Gail suggested. At the café Beth basked in her family's attention. She ordered a slab of chocolate mud cake with her coffee, and as she smoothed cream over the icing, Beth silently thanked God for helping her make the right choice. There was no way she would have entered the eisteddfod if she had been five and a half months pregnant.

Libby: 23 weeks

Libby lay in the bath and watched her unborn baby play. Her belly button had popped upwards a few weeks ago and now it looked like the tip of a buried shell, marking the end of the shadowy *linea nigra* like an 'X' on a treasure map. She ran through a mental checklist of names. Tara, Tatum, Taylor – she seemed to be going through a 'T' phase. For a boy she liked Tate or perhaps Toby. Darren said people called dogs Toby, but people called dogs all sorts of things.

A limb jabbed her just above the pubic bone and Libby stared. It was weird seeing bits of arms or legs jut out of her tummy. Like that movie, *Alien*. Then the doubts began again. What if her baby was disabled in some way? Would she still love it? She shivered and turned on the hot tap. Surely God wouldn't be that cruel.

That night Libby was restless. She read the newspaper in bed and learnt that it was the spring equinox, the time when night was the same length as day. The thought made her feel small. Libby lit a mosquito coil and took a cup of hot chocolate onto the balcony. The moon was waning and the evening star led her gaze to the river. There must be millions of pregnant women out there, she thought. Perhaps some were watching the same star as her.

Libby flipped through the newspaper, reading by streetlight. The evening was calm, but the weather chart showed a ridge of low pressure building up in the Indian Ocean. She read her horoscope, then skimmed over the other signs. Aquarius. Her baby was going to be an Aquarian, unless it came late. Aquarians were going to have an unsettled week according to the paper. Libby wondered whether it counted if you were still in the womb. Depends on whether you believe in predestiny, she decided. As Libby licked the last drops of chocolate from the side of her cup, she gazed at the river and tried to decide whether this pregnancy was part of God's plan for her or just bad luck.

The next day Libby borrowed an astrology book from the local library and looked up January thirty-first. *Freedom loving by nature*, it said, *those born under the sign of the water bearer tend to be individualistic, dedicated and friendly.* Libby had never taken much notice of star signs. It seemed bizarre that the population could be divided into twelve groups and it certainly didn't tie in with her Catholic upbringing. But Britt had explained that a person's sun sign was only one indicator. The moon, ascendant and other planets were equally important in understanding yourself and how others saw you.

Libby read on. *If you're a water-bearer you are a fixed air sign. You tend to resonate towards Uranus and favour the practical rather than dreams and yearnings.*

'Well, better an engineer than a poet I guess,' Libby muttered. 'At least that's what baby's grandpa Erikson would say.' She frowned and looked up her own star sign, Aries.

Fiercely independent and proud, your optimistic faith carries you through the harsh realities of life. A cardinal fire sign, you are confident and have the courage to fight for what you believe in.

That last bit certainly fits me at the moment, Libby thought, wondering what a cardinal fire sign was. But she hadn't always had the courage to stand up for her beliefs. It was a new thing. Part of becoming pregnant and having to grow up. And as for confidence, that was all on the surface. Once she'd decided to keep the baby she *had* to convince people that she was capable. Besides, falling into a heap would prove her mother right.

**

Ashleigh banged on the door the next day. 'It's pouring outside,' she said, dripping all over the floor. Libby handed her some dry socks and a jumper, then showed her the book.

'Yep, that's like you,' Ashleigh said. 'Always resonating towards Uranus.' Libby punched her. 'Sorry, I couldn't resist,' Ashleigh laughed. 'But you have always been confident. Remember that time at primary school when you saved our team at the interschool debating competition? And how about when you stood up to Billy the Bruiser?'

Libby grinned. 'That's right. I'd forgotten about him. But I'm not really confident. Not inside,' she argued.

'Well, you're a good actor then,' Ashleigh said. 'Does it say that you should be on the stage?'

'Yep, destined for fame. Brilliant voice and looks ...' Libby pretended to read.

'Yeah, sure. Stop dreaming. What does it say about me?'

'July ninth. What does that make you? Cancer?'

'Mmm, it usually says I'm a boring homebody.'

'*Home-loving ...*'

'Same thing. I wish I was a Sagittarian. They're meant to be wild.'

'Hang on, it also says that you're *sensitive ...*'

'Boring!' Ashleigh squealed.

'And that *the soft creature inside your shell is artistic and visionary.*'

'That sounds a bit better. I wouldn't mind being artistic. But that should be yours. You're the musical one.'

'Not lately.'

'I was wondering how you felt about leaving the choir. Britt reckons Mr B lost it last week. "You'll have to learn to stop hiding behind Elisabeth McCrae's voice now",' Ashleigh imitated.

'Did he really say that?'

'Mmhmm, or so Britt said. Anyway the choir's pretty hopeless without you.'

'I doubt it.'

'So are you singing here on your own?'

'Not really. I'm not doing much cello either. The music's dried up. Perhaps the baby's taken all the extra space inside me.'

Libby seemed sad, so Ashleigh changed the subject. 'Let's look up someone else,' she suggested. 'When's Darren's birthday?'

'He's a Pisces. A vague but sensitive dreamer.'

'Yeah, that'd be right. What about Sasha? Remember she had that big party in November? She must be Scorpio.'

'What does it say about her?'

Ashleigh read for a few moments, then closed the book. 'You don't want to know,' she said.

Darren and Sasha seemed to be getting on like a house on fire. Beth knew it was sick to follow them around. She hated herself for doing it, but she couldn't help it. Their happiness fascinated her. She memorised Sasha's timetable and was often at the lockers just before she arrived. She knew which day Sasha ordered lunch and even what she ate. One wholemeal salad roll – with no onion – and a small strawberry milk. Sometimes she'd have an iceblock or a donut but that was rare.

Darren was devoted to her. Had he been that way with Beth? She couldn't remember. After a while Britt made stalking jokes and even Ashleigh tried to warn her off. 'People are talking,' she said.

'I'm not following them. She just has a similar timetable to mine.'

'What about lunchtimes?'

'It's a free world. Can't I order lunch sometimes?'

'You hardly ever used to.'

'Well I do now.' Beth hated herself for snapping. Britt and Tran had pretty much given up on her. She didn't want to lose Ashleigh too.

Hanging round the library began by accident. She was returning books one day when she discovered that a desk by the window had a bird's-eye view of the seniors' area. From there she could watch Darren and his girlfriend as much as she liked and not be accused of spying. Beth also liked browsing in the human biology section. There was a fat text on pregnancy which seemed to wink at her whenever she passed. She huddled behind the tall shelves, flicking through the pages, feasting on sketches of wombs, foetuses and swollen bellies. One day, as the siren rang, she grabbed some books and took the pile to the counter.

'This should be helpful for our project on reproduction,' she gushed to the Year Eight library monitor. The girl smiled and zapped the bar codes.

Beth stuffed the books into her bag, then hurried over to the lockers. She was so engrossed that she almost bumped into Darren.

'What a surprise,' Sasha muttered sarcastically. 'Here you are again.' Someone behind them snickered and Beth blushed as one of the library books fell out of her bag. She scrambled to collect it but not before the other girls had a good gawk at the title.

'*Diary of a Pregnancy*,' one of them whispered. Beth froze.

'Caught out badly,' she heard someone mutter as people snickered. Beth was ready to bolt when Darren picked up the book and handed it to her.

'Let me know when your aunt has her baby,' he said loudly.

'What? Oh yeah, of course,' she mumbled. 'Thanks.' Sasha gave Beth a foul look and linked arms with Darren.

'Better hurry or you'll be late for English,' she told him. Darren glanced at Beth's tummy then bounded upstairs while Beth turned and walked the other way, feeling stupid and angry. 'Idiot,' she told herself. 'Why can't you just get over it?'

Libby: 25 weeks

'I wish I could do the exams somewhere else. I'm dreading turning up at school like this. I feel so obvious. Can you imagine the look I'll get from Sister Greenbushes? And I don't know what to wear. These preggie dresses make me look like an elephant. Everyone will stare their heads off.'

'Come on, Libby. It's not such a big deal and the other kids know anyway.'

'Yeah, but seeing is believing. And there's a lot to see.'

'It won't make any difference to the people who matter,' Ashleigh said.

'That's easy to say. If you had a belly like this you'd feel differently.'

'Probably,' Ashleigh sniffed. 'I was only trying to help.'

'Yeah I know. Hey look, I'm sorry.' Libby hugged her. 'I'm just nervous about seeing everyone. Or having them see me. And I'll probably flunk the exams anyway.'

'Well if you keep saying that, you probably will! You got good marks in your assignments. Better than me.'

'Not history.'

'At least you're not failing anything! Look, if I can pass maths, you'll romp home in history. But if you don't stop being such a martyr, I'm going home. I get enough whingeing from Dad.'

'How is your dad?'

'He's pretty down actually. "On the scrap heap at forty-eight, who would have thought it …"' Ashleigh droned.

'Can't he get another job?'

'He's trying. The job agency reckons he's over qualified.'

'How can you be over qualified?'

'They said managers don't want to hire people with two degrees.'

'Why not?'

'Clever people make them nervous. They have to watch their backs.'

'So what's he going to do?'

'Who knows? Mum's got another job. Three evenings a week she calls people trying to convince them to change phone companies …'

'Oh, no. I got stuck with one of them last week. I couldn't escape until I'd heard about all the latest flexi-plans.'

'Yeah, she hates it, but she reckons there's no choice. Not until Dad finds something. Anyway, I'd better go. I need to memorise some philosophical quotes to sprinkle into my essays. Will you be okay tomorrow?'

'Yeah, I'll turn up at the last minute and make an entrance,' Libby joked. Neither of them laughed.

'Why don't you come via my place,' Ashleigh said. 'We can go together.'

'Aren't you embarrassed to be seen with me?'

'Don't be stupid,' Ashleigh replied. 'As if the rest of us are angels. We just didn't get caught.'

'Thanks,' Libby replied. 'I'd feel better walking in with someone.'

**

The phone rang as Ashleigh left. It was Gail calling to wish Libby good luck and to ask whether she wanted to come over for dinner.

'I'm in the middle of studying,' Libby lied, 'and I've still got some of the soup you sent over.'

'You need a good dinner so that you can concentrate tomorrow.'

'I know, Mum. I've got cold chicken and salad as well. It's okay, I just feel like leftovers tonight.'

'All right. Do you need a lift in the morning?'

'No, it's okay. I can catch the eight-ten bus from here. It connects with the one that runs along The Boulevard. Ashleigh and I are going to meet outside her place and go together.'

'Let me know if you get stuck and I'll come and get you.'

'Thanks, Mum. I'll be fine.'

'Okay. Good luck.'

'Thanks, 'bye.' Libby took out her English notes but she couldn't concentrate. She poured herself a glass of juice and took it onto the verandah. Cars were parked all over the verge below. Something was on at the foreshore. Huge kites filled the sky.

Libby pulled on her boots and went to join the crowd. It was a good day for kites — windy, but not too gusty. She stopped beside a man with an enormous jellyfish kite. He'd taken off his shirt and Libby watched his shoulders as he struggled to control the kite strings.

'D'you want to try it?' he asked.

'I don't know what to do.'

'It's easy,' he laughed. 'You just need to concentrate.' He glanced at Libby's belly. 'Here, I'll keep hold of one side of the controls and you take the other.'

Libby reached out and felt the kite tug her arm. 'What do I do now?'

'Just enjoy it. Look!' Their kite was flirting with a Chinese dragon. 'Okay, now let's make it dip.' He showed her how to change direction, and the jellyfish lunged.

'This is great,' Libby squealed, then she noticed two boys watching. 'I think someone else wants a go,' she said.

The man called them over. 'I'm Nathan,' he said, brushing her hand as he took the controls.

'Thanks, Nathan. That was excellent,' Libby replied. 'I'm Libby.'

Nathan smiled. 'Maybe I'll see you around, Libby.'

Libby walked home, feeling young for the first time in months. Nathan the kite man must have seen that she was pregnant, yet it didn't seem to bother him. A vision of Darren's face bubbled into her mind and Libby firmly squashed it.

**

After staring into the sky, the flat felt like a shoebox. Libby paced around the lounge room feeling trapped. She sat down to look at her notes, then stood up and paced again. Then she took out all the clothes she could still squeeze into and lay them over the bed. She wanted to wear something bright to the exams, but the maternity gear was either dark colours or pastel pinks and blues. Like babies, Libby thought. She put tops over dresses and lay different combinations together. It was obvious that she was *anticipating a blessed event*. If she was going to turn up at school, she may as well do it in style.

Libby took out her sewing box and dumped ribbons and patches over the baggy windcheaters her mum had loaned her. She sketched a few patterns onto paper, then cut shapes out of fabric scraps to embroider onto the clothes. Libby loved sewing but hadn't had much time lately.

As she pinned shapes onto the clothes and began sewing, she felt herself relaxing. Two hours later her mother's green windcheater had beetles walking across it and another blue top was covered in jellyfish. Libby found some old fabric colour, dyed swirls onto a pair of leggings, then hung them out to dry. Later she could add fish shapes and maybe some seaweedy strands running up her calves. She stretched and looked at the clock. Time for dinner.

Libby took the cold chook and salad out of the fridge, then sat down to read her English notes. She'd spent ages sewing, but it had been worth it. She'd feel more confident walking into the exams in these clothes. Just because she was pregnant, she didn't have to look frumpy.

Beth still hadn't been to mass. Each Sunday Gail alternated between reproachful glances and nagging. Two days before the first exam she sat on the end of Beth's bed. 'I know you don't want to hear this, but please listen anyway.' She paused. 'I'm worried that you won't do as well as you can without going to confession.' Beth opened her mouth to protest, but her mother was well prepared. 'Just listen for a moment. All year I've been praying that you'll do well. You've worked hard and I know God has listened. But how can He truly help when you haven't been to confession for so long?'

Emotional blackmail, Beth thought. 'I haven't had time,' she replied.

'Some things are more important than others,' Gail chided. 'If I drive you down, we can be back within half an hour. Surely that won't make any difference to your studies.'

Beth knew she had to go back to church sometime. She *wanted* to go back. This was the longest she'd ever missed confession, and living a lie of innocence made her feel hypocritical. Maybe her mum was right; letting her guilt fester wasn't helping anyone.

'Okay,' Beth said. 'But don't worry about giving me a lift. I need the exercise.' She closed her textbook. 'I'll go now.'

Gail beamed and hugged her. 'You're a good girl,' she whispered. 'You deserve to do well. God sees that and so do I.' Beth felt like a fraud. Gail may think she was a good girl, but no doubt God saw things differently. She hoped Father Patrick would be busy with a christening or a funeral, but the church was quiet. Beth entered the confessional booth and waited. A few minutes later the other door opened and Father Patrick sat down. She recognised his asthmatic breathing.

'Forgive me, Father, for I have sinned.'

'Yes, my child.'

Beth closed her eyes. Father Patrick would surely recognise her voice. She silently asked for courage. An image of the Madonna and child filled Beth's mind, calming her, until she looked into Mary's eyes and saw Marina's pain. Then the babe in Mary's arms turned to stare at Beth with the vengeful eyes of Gabriel, the abortion protester. Beth gasped. What had she done?

'My child?'

Beth tried to control her breathing. 'I'm sorry, Father.'

'Take your time ...' But Beth couldn't do it.

'Forgive me, Father,' she mumbled, as she opened the door and fled into the sunshine. Beth ran until she came to the park. Then she sat on the swing and cried.

**

'I bet that feels better,' Gail said as Beth closed the back door.

'I've decided not to go any more,' Beth answered quietly.

Gail stopped stirring the soup. 'Not to go where?'

104

'To church.'

'But, darling ...'

'I'm sorry, Mum. It just doesn't feel right.'

'How can it not feel right?'

'I don't know. It just doesn't.'

'What will I tell Father Patrick?' Gail asked.

'Is that all that matters?' Beth shouted. 'Is Father Patrick's opinion more important than my immortal soul?'

'Of course not, Beth. It's just that ...'

'All this trotting off to mass and confessing every week. Why can't I talk to God at the beach or while I'm walking in the park?'

'You can, Beth. You know that. It's just ...'

'Just what?'

'The church is our community. Where we meet our friends. People who believe. Others like us.'

'So I can't have friends who don't believe?'

'Beth, stop trying to start an argument. I've never questioned your choice of friends. I think Ashleigh is a lovely girl.'

'And what about Britt and Tran?'

'I don't know them as well,' Gail said defensively. 'They don't come over as often as Ashleigh does.'

'And their parents aren't Catholic.'

'Your friends are all welcome. You know that.' Beth sniffed.

'But it's not just that is it?' Gail continued. 'You've changed.' She turned away. 'I don't understand your reasons. You used to enjoy coming to church. But it's your decision. You're old enough to choose.'

Beth stomped into her room and flung her stuffed bear off the bed. She was so fed up. She loved going to church. The stone walls and quiet atmosphere calmed her. But she couldn't go now. Not after today. While she was studying, she'd managed to avoid giving her parents a reason. How could she tell her mother that their prayers reminded her of zealots chanting outside a clinic?

**

Beth was able to forget about Darren, lost babies, mortal sin and guilt until the last exam. The reading time was over and all around her pens were scribbling.

Abortion is murder. Murder the murderers! The face of Gabriel was twisted around the words on the exam booklet in front of her. His nose hooked over question three and his eyes, fanatically green, blocked the diagram in question one. He was trying to spit up at her but gravity was against him. Concentrate, she told herself. You need to pass this to get into music. Concentrate. But Marina's voice was floating amongst the words. *Bastards, pricks, bastards. They should parade in front of my uncle's office …*

Beth shook her head. Concentrate!

The supervisor walked over. 'Are you all right, Elisabeth?' It was Mr Simms, her English teacher. Beth smiled. 'Yes, of course, just a little tired.'

Mr Simms gave her a sympathetic smile. 'Two hours and it'll all be over. Take a deep breath and try again. You'll be fine.' If this was English she would be. Beth knew she'd done well on that exam. The thought encouraged her and she blocked Marina's voice. 'After the exam,' she muttered. 'I'll think about you after the exam. I promise.'

But after the exam, Beth ran to Ashleigh's house. There was a note taped to the door. *Gone to Mario's for a hamburger and coffee with the girls. Meet you there.* Beth guessed that 'the girls' meant Britt and Tran.

Since she'd missed the forests concert, Beth knew they'd been gossiping. They were always watching her. Taking mental notes to compare later. But she was sick of moping around feeling guilty, and of being alone. Now that her last exam was over she wanted to muck around and be silly, like they used to. She sat on Ashleigh's front step and closed her eyes. Then she forced herself to visualise Gabriel's face. 'You don't know anything about me,' she hissed. 'I'm not ready to be a mother, and when I am ready to bring a baby into this world, I want it to come to a home where two adults, in a stable relationship, can give it all the love it deserves.' Gabriel sneered as he began to fade. 'Besides,' Beth added. 'Only God has the right to judge. Not you.' Gabriel fizzled into insignificance as Beth wondered if that was what she really believed.

She stood up and wandered into Ashleigh's back yard. Their old tree house was still there, perched in the pepper tree's knotty arms. Beth remembered the fun and secrets they'd shared up there. Then, on impulse, she used the knotted rope to swing into the branches.

The deck was warm. Beth lay on her back watching patterns of sunlight filter through the leaves, and tried to work out what exactly she was punishing herself for. Was she truly shamed to have taken a life, or was she feeling guilty because of Father Patrick and her parents?

Beth closed her eyes. Surely it was wrong for a child to live in a hostile body for nine months and then be met by a mother who resented it stealing her youth. What kind of start was that?

Beth shook her head. There were so many studies linking criminal behaviour to despair and poverty in the early years. A mother's unconditional loving welcome was too important a gift to deny a child, but then, so was life. On one level, Beth believed the church teachings. She had denied a life. That was wrong, and yet she also believed passionately that it was her right to decide. It wasn't Father Patrick's, or her mother's or father's choice. It was hers. And if she had to choose again, Beth would follow the same path. She knew in her bones that she'd made the right choice for her, so why couldn't she let go of the guilt?

Beth sighed and tried to imagine an eight-week-old embryo. She smiled. It was a funny looking thing, but she could see its little heart beating strongly. She focused on that heart and imagined cradling the tiny being. As she wrapped love around it, the name Danni came to mind. She whispered it aloud.

'I'm sorry, Danni,' Beth mumbled. She sat up and looked into the sunlight until tears streamed down her cheeks. Then she fumbled in her bag for a tissue and found Ashleigh's note. Did it really matter if Britt and Tran talked about her? Isn't that what friends did when they were worried? And she had been totally unpredictable lately. She looked up through the leaves one last time, then swung down on the rope and walked towards Mario's.

**

108

Beth hovered by the door and looked around.

'Hi, we weren't sure if you'd come,' Ashleigh called.

Tran looked surprised, then she stood up and grabbed another chair. 'You look different,' she said, giving Beth a hug. 'Is everything okay?'

Beth smiled. Tran was always so perceptive. 'I'm fine,' she said. 'At least I think I am. It feels like something's shifted inside me.'

'It's the old Beth resurfacing. I was wondering when she'd break free.'

Beth stiffened, but then relaxed. Something *had* shifted. The exams were over. She'd probably done okay, so hopefully she'd be at uni soon. What difference did Tran's comments make now? There was only one more thing to worry about: her university interview. To get into UWA she had to have an audition. Beth knew she'd be nervous when the time came, but now she just wanted to relax. Her progressive music score from school was good and she practised cello every morning. The highly commended from the eisteddfod should help, and if that wasn't enough ... well perhaps it wasn't meant to be.

Beth smiled as Britt moved her chair to make room at the table. She'd made it through the year. She wasn't six months pregnant. Her friends were happy to see her. What more did she want? She threw her books onto the floor and sat down. Britt laughed. 'Welcome back to the world. It's good to see you, but I have to say, Darren Erikson wasn't worth all that drama.'

Beth grinned at her friends. Then she looked across at Ashleigh. 'You're right,' she said softly. 'He has his good points, but he definitely wasn't worth the pain.'

Libby: 27 weeks

Libby flung off the sheet and sat up in bed. The toddler's face was so vivid. A flossy little girl with huge blue eyes and Scandinavian white-blond hair. She was dressed in a pinafore with old-fashioned petticoats flouncing below the hem. They were walking towards a park holding hands. The toddler's chubby fingers curled tightly around Libby's hand. There were pelicans ahead. They scared the girl and she didn't want to let go of her mummy.

Her mummy! Libby put a hand over her belly and stared into the night. The little girl didn't want to let go of her mummy. Suddenly Libby knew that her baby was a girl. A daughter with clear blue eyes. Libby tucked the blankets around her tummy and hugged the secret. Knowing that it was a girl pleased her.

**

The weekends had become better, although spending so much time together had taken some of the romance out of their relationship.

'Dr Wong reckons I should eat plenty of fruit and drink lots of water,' Libby told Darren one Saturday as she unpacked bags of bananas and apples. 'She said a lot of women get constipated during pregnancy. Apples are s'posed to be the best. They've got heaps of roughage.'

Darren turned away. Why did she have to go on about the details? It was hard enough to feel romantic with her leaking breasts and massive belly. He didn't need to hear about her bum as well.

**

If the weather was fine, Libby began the day with a walk. Sometimes she strolled under the highway into Kings Park. Other days she wandered along the foreshore. At the end of each walk Libby sat for a while on the jetty at the end of her street. She loved dangling her legs over the edge watching umbrella shaped jellyfish drift through the water like some endlessly changing screen saver. As she sat there, Libby thought about her baby. The idea of giving birth scared her, but she looked forward to meeting the child that she carried.

Now that the exams had finished she often met her friends by the river. Libby's twenty-seventh week seemed a good enough reason to celebrate, so Ashleigh had arranged a brunch at the park. Libby wandered along the cycle path and waved to Tran and Britt. 'Where's Ashleigh?' she asked, putting down her basket.

'Close your eyes,' Britt ordered.

'Why?'

'Just do it!' They laughed and held their hands over Libby's eyes. 'Okay, you can open them now.'

Libby looked and saw Ashleigh wheeling a pram with large old-fashioned wheels. Her dog-eared teddy from home was dressed in a bright jacket and sat on the tiny quilt inside. 'It's for you,' Ashleigh said. 'The kids at school put in for it. Some of the teachers donated too. All the names are on the card.'

'But these prams cost a fortune.'

Her friends looked smug. 'Do you like it?' they asked.

Libby hugged them. 'What do you reckon? I love it! Thank you so much, guys.'

They showed her how to fold up the pram and adjust the seat. Then Tran tucked Old Ted under the covers and they took him for a stroll along the foreshore.

'This is a great area to live in,' Britt said as a pelican skimmed to a landing on the water.

'Yeah, it's working out really well,' Libby replied.

'When's Darren moving in?'

'In two weeks.'

'You still reckon it'll work?'

'Tran!'

'What? I won't be able to ask after he's moved in, will I?'

Libby smiled. 'I don't know,' she admitted. 'The flat feels like it's mine. It's great having him stay on weekends, but … it'll be different when he moves in.'

Britt bounced the pram over the grass and balanced Old Ted on a swing. 'It must be odd,' she said, 'you know, having a baby growing inside you.'

'Yep, it sure is.'

'Everything's happening too quickly,' Britt continued. 'I don't want us all to change. We'll still see each other next year, won't we?'

'Of course,' Ashleigh agreed, while Libby and Tran stared at the grass.

112

School was over and freedom was around the corner. Beth had waited years for this day. Now that it was here, she felt a bit let down, but mainly relieved. She was ready for a change — hanging out to get to uni and re-invent herself.

By some alphabetical quirk of fate Darren was seated directly in front of her for their farewell assembly. Beth studied the twin whorls on the back of his head as she waited for her name to be called. She'd never noticed that he had a double crown. Strange. She could have been the mother of a double-crowned child. Beth thought back to that day at the beach, and wondered where she'd be now if she'd made a different decision. Then she remembered that moment in the tree house. Besides being rounder, would she be a different person? Would she be happier? She doubted it.

The wind whipped a strand of Darren's hair loose from his ponytail. She was tempted to tuck it into place for him. What would Sasha think of that? For the first time since May, Beth felt okay about him. They were partners in the mistake, and he'd been pretty good about it really. Better than most of the Year Twelve boys would have been. At least he hadn't told anyone.

As if sensing her thoughts, Darren turned and caught her watching him. Beth froze. Caught out again, she thought. 'Can I talk to you afterwards?' he whispered. Beth ignored Nicola listening beside her and nodded. Darren smiled and turned back to the assembly. They were up to 'D'. It was nearly his turn.

Beth watched Darren walk across the asphalt to collect his certificate. In one way it was a pity, she thought. He had great genes to pass on. Then she looked down the row of seats towards Ashleigh. She was a good mate. Beth knew the others would probably have dropped her if it wasn't for Ashleigh. Not that she'd have blamed them. It had been a strange year.

More names were called, then it was her turn. 'Elisabeth McCrae,' the principal announced.

Beth adjusted her skirt and walked to the dais. Her last day at school. The beginning of a new life. At last.

**

The graduating students served tea and coffee to the parents and guests, then they hoovered into the biscuits. Beth grabbed one of the last Tim-Tams and noticed Darren looking her way. She walked towards the toilet block and waited under a tree for him to follow. He looked nervous as he sat down beside her.

'Congratulations,' Beth said. He seemed surprised. 'On finishing Year Twelve,' she continued.

'Oh yeah, thanks. You too.'

She watched some ants dragging away a dead beetle and waited for him to begin.

'Umm, you know a few weeks ago, when you dropped that book ...'

Beth blushed. 'Yeah, hey thanks for covering for me.

And also for the money. I never said anything, but I knew it was from you.'

'I'm glad you got it. I wasn't sure.'

'I should have said something. I'm sorry, I guess I haven't been very, umm … thoughtful.'

'That's okay. I probably could have handled it better too.'

'Did you want to talk about something?'

'Yeah, I've been wanting to speak to you for ages, but you know, it's hard with Sash and everything.'

'You two seem happy.' Beth couldn't help the touch of sarcasm in her voice.

'Well, it's okay. But what I was wondering though, I mean, you don't have to talk about it if you don't want to. I just need to know. Well, I'd *like* to know … What actually happened? I promise I won't tell anyone.'

'What about Sasha?'

'Especially not Sasha. She'd kill me.'

Beth took a deep breath. 'You know that day you were waiting for me?' Darren nodded. 'I'd been into town. I had an abortion.'

Darren stared at the ground. 'I'm really sorry,' he muttered. 'I should have gone with you. If you'd told me, I would have.'

Beth touched his arm. It was warm from the sun. 'I know,' she said, 'but I was angry and wanted to go alone.'

'Was the money enough to pay for it? Was it covered by Medicare or anything?'

'Pretty much,' Beth lied. She didn't want to tell him about the false name.

'I guess it was painful?'

'It wasn't so much the pain, though that was bad

115

enough. It was the guilt. I know I did the right thing. For me and the baby. And Mum and Dad. And even you. But for a long time, part of me felt really guilty.' Darren was quiet as Beth shrugged. 'But hey, don't worry. Catholics are trained for that since birth.'

'And what about now?' Darren asked. Beth thought for a moment, wondering whether to tell him about the feeling in the tree house, but she decided against it. That was something between her and 'Danni'. She smiled at Darren and touched his arm.

'I think I'm okay now,' she said quietly. Two of Darren's mates turned the corner and Beth pulled away her hand, knowing she must look guilty, but Darren didn't seem to care who saw them.

'Did you end up putting UWA as your first choice?' he asked.

Beth nodded. 'I went for the interview and audition last week.'

'How did you go?'

'The audition went well. I chose the same piece that I played at the eisteddfod and they seemed to like it. I don't know about the interview though. When they asked me what I saw as my career goals, I went blank. I should have studied the career options part of their prospectus more carefully.'

'So what did you end up saying?'

'I can't remember exactly. Something about being a musical director for theatre.'

'Well, that's better than saying music teaching. I bet everyone says that.'

'I'd be a hopeless teacher. I'm not patient enough. How about you?' Beth asked. 'What did you put for your first choice?'

'Science at UWA. I'm still trying to decide between Marine Science and Phys Ed, but then I met this guy who's doing a philosophy major in Arts and it sounds really good. If I do Phys Ed I might be able to sub-major in philosophy.'

'I was thinking about doing philosophy too.'

Darren laughed. 'I might see you in class then.' He stood up and held out a hand to help her. 'I know I'm not your favourite person, but it would be nice if we could be friends.'

Beth smiled. He was still holding her hand. 'I'd like that,' she said. 'It would be nice to see a familiar face on campus.' They walked back to the others. Beth laughed when she saw Nicola staring at them. Her mouth had dropped open.

'Careful you don't catch a fly,' Beth whispered as they walked by.

Libby: 29 weeks

Darren felt that he'd done well with his exams, all except English anyway. As soon as school finished, he packed his bags and moved in with Libby. At first it was great. There was no one to tell them what to eat and when to go to bed. Not that they weren't keen to do that. With a bun already in the oven, they made the most of the contraception-free time. And with Libby's belly in the way, they even learnt to be creative.

There were shy times too. Sharing a bathroom. Accepting that there was more than one way to dry dishes and squeeze toothpaste. Getting undressed in front of each other was a novelty after their previous gropes in the dark, and Libby tried to get used to having to share her bed.

They had parties when some of the kids from school came over. The neighbours complained, but they ignored them. It was fun for a while, but by the third party, Libby felt like they were being used. She was tired of mopping up beer and finding couples she barely knew on the floor in the morning. She started locking the door and pretending they were out.

On quiet evenings they watched TV or sat in the kitchen playing board games. Monopoly was their favourite. As they mortgaged properties and went to jail, they laughed at each other's suggestions for baby names.

'It can't be Max,' Darren insisted. 'We had a cat called Max and it was useless!'

'Jack's no good either. Grandma had a dog called Jack and it was always going for it on someone's leg.'

Despite Libby's worries, they seemed to be getting along okay. Darren was often out with his mates and that gave Libby space to herself. She enjoyed the time on her own. Gail had given them some pot plants. One was a young Norfolk Island pine, and in between embroidering ducks onto socks and singlets, Libby sewed sequins onto ornaments so she could transform the pine into a Christmas tree.

They took each day one at a time, and there was an unspoken agreement not to mention words like 'commitment'. Both sets of parents were disappointed, but was harder for Darren's mum and dad to understand Libby's decision. They weren't religious, but they thought she was a modern-day Jezebel who'd trapped their only son. Meanwhile Libby's father was furious at Darren for taking advantage of his little girl and not using a condom.

'In this day and age ...' he raged. 'What with hepatitis and AIDS. Don't you kids listen to the news? There are epidemics, in case you hadn't noticed.'

'Neither of us had been with anyone else,' Libby mumbled.

'*You* might not have,' her dad replied bitterly, before storming off. 'I don't know about him ...'

But her father was wrong. Libby knew Darren had been a virgin. But he was right about the condom. She'd thought Darren would have organised that. Despite their health teacher's assurances, some boys still reckoned girls who carried condoms were slack.

119

Somewhere deep inside, Libby also felt that Darren had let her down.

**

The antenatal appointments were fortnightly now.

'Dr Wong reckons I can have an ultrasound if I want to,' she told Darren one evening.

'Do you want to?'

'Of course. She reckons the baby's legally viable now.'

'Meaning?'

'It's become a person. Whatever happens now, it has to be registered. So, do you want to come along?'

'To the ultrasound?'

'Yeah.'

'Okay. When is it?'

'She said she can fit us in tomorrow afternoon, at three o'clock.'

**

Dr Wong's surgery was peaceful. Stepping in from the road was like entering another world. Chinese scrolls and baby photos decorated the walls and there were always fresh flowers on the reception desk. After helping Libby settle, Darren watched the other women reading magazines. They were all much older than Libby.

Libby had been told to drink two litres of water before coming in. 'If she doesn't hurry I'm going to wet myself,' she hissed after twenty minutes. As Darren stood up to ask how much longer, the receptionist called them in. He followed Libby into a small room that smelt of herbs. Some combination of lavender and lemon grass perhaps. Libby whispered that Dr Wong was interested in the effects of aromatherapy during labour.

'Hello, I'm Dr Wong, you must be Darren.' Darren nodded and shook the extended hand. Despite the tiny size of Dr Wong's palm, her grip was firm. Good for catching babies, Darren thought.

Dr Wong showed him the ultrasound machine, then she covered Libby's belly with some jelly-like stuff. As she eased the sensor over Libby's bulge, a blurry image appeared on the monitor. It looked like craters on the moon. 'Can you see the head?' Dr Wong asked.

Libby nodded excitedly while Darren stared at the screen. He tried to think creatively, but what he thought was the baby's head ended up being its bottom. Dr Wong pointed out the legs and arms, and after a few minutes Darren began to understand the shape. He watched the tiny chest rise.

'Hey, it's breathing,' he cried. 'I can see it's chest going up and down.'

Dr Wong laughed. 'It's exciting isn't it?' she said, but Darren was silent. That fuzzy thing was his baby. For the first time it seemed real. He grinned at Libby.

'Do you want to know its sex?' Dr Wong asked. Libby shook her head. She knew it was a girl, and for the moment she wanted to keep the secret to herself. Dr Wong looked at Darren. 'Whatever Libby wants,' he said.

Dr Wong waited for a clear view, then printed out a copy of the scan.

'He looks like a cartoon figure caught in fog,' Darren

said as they sat in a café staring at their kid's first photo.

'Do you think it's a boy?' she asked.

Darren blushed. 'I don't know,' he mumbled. 'A boy would be good.' Libby smiled, rested her hands on her secret and ordered a cappuccino.

'I can't believe we've really finished,' Ashleigh said. 'Finished school at last. No more assignments, no more teachers, no more sirens interrupting lunch ...'

'No more history. No more uniforms!' They were at Ashleigh's house painting their toenails. Ashleigh had been going on about Spud again. Beth didn't want to hear another word about his *amazing brown eyes*, so she tried to change the subject. 'What do you want to do today?' she asked.

'Just hang around.'

'We did that yesterday. Let's go into town and see a movie.'

'Which one?'

'I don't care.'

'I can't really afford it.'

'Why don't we just go into town then? We could look at the shops, or go to the art gallery, or Kings Park.'

'Yeah, that's a good idea.'

'Which one?'

'Kings Park. I haven't been there for ages. It'd be nice to go for a walk. We could get off the bus near the tennis courts and cut across that bush path to the bluff.'

'And have a coffee at the lookout.'

'Then walk down the steps into town.'

'Sounds good.'

Ashleigh looked at the timetable above her desk. 'C'mon,' she said, 'there's a bus in ten minutes. If we miss that, we'll have to wait half an hour for the next one.'

Beth grabbed her bag and hat. 'I'm ready,' she said. 'Let's go.'

**

'Hey, what's that over there?' Ashleigh asked.

Beth shrugged. 'Looks like a café. Want to go over?'

'Okay.' They followed the road beside the tennis club.

'We used to come here when James was on trainer wheels. He loved whizzing round the bike track. The rest was all parkland then.'

'Want to go in?'

'Might as well. I'm ready for a coffee.'

The café opened onto a huge playground. Although it was early, there were mobs of mothers and kids. They walked past the climbing forts towards a maze made out of pipes. 'Look at this,' Ashleigh said. 'Kids have got it made these days.'

'So have the parents,' Beth replied, nodding to the tables. Mums sipped coffee while their kids ran wild within the safety of the fenced yard.

'Does it make you feel weird?' Ashleigh asked.

'What do you mean?'

'You know, that could have been you.'

'No way.' But as they took their cappuccinos to an outside table, Beth turned her chair so that she was facing the car park.

They walked into town along the Terrace, then

wandered through the malls. Hanging around, checking out the guys and fashions without thinking they should be studying was such a luxury.

'D'you want to go to the gallery?' Beth asked.

'Let's eat first. I'm starving.'

'I've only got a few dollars.'

'Me too, but there's a place in Northbridge where you can eat all you like for five dollars.'

'Five dollars?'

'Yeah, it's some religious group. Hare Krishnas I think.'

'Sounds a bit suss. What's in the food?'

'Just vegies. There's no meat, but it's okay, I've been there before. They're not pushy or anything. They just give you a few pamphlets to take away.'

'Okay, let's try it.'

They sat beneath an enigmatic photo of a guru. 'Mum would have a fit if she saw me here,' Beth mumbled between mouthfuls.

'Do you think? Permaculture's not exactly mainstream. She probably meets lots of different people.'

'Permaculture may not be mainstream, but her friends are. Believe me, she'd have a fit.' Ashleigh wasn't convinced, but she didn't say anything. As they waited in line to pay, Beth read the noticeboard. 'What's ear-candling?' she whispered. Ashleigh shrugged as Beth kept reading. 'Yoga, Tai Chi, meditation ... They've got classes in everything. Why don't we go along to something? It says first sessions are free.'

Ashleigh looked through the pamphlets. 'Okay. You choose one and I'll choose one.'

'Aromatherapy,' Beth said.

'Aromatherapy?'

'Yeah, you know, mixing scented oils. I've always wanted to learn about that.'

'Okay … and I'll choose ear-candling. Nah, only joking. How about … *An Introduction to Buddhism*? Or would that be too strange for you?'

Beth remembered the fiasco at the confessional. 'No, I reckon that would be interesting,' she said. 'Where do they hold the classes?'

'Upstairs on Saturday afternoons. The aromatherapy is on Tuesday evenings.'

'Do you want to ask Britt and Tran?'

'They'd probably like the aromatherapy, but I don't think Tran needs an *Introduction to Buddhism* course.'

Beth smiled. 'She'll laugh when we tell her.'

Libby: 31 weeks

Libby saw the ad on the noticeboard of the health shop when she went to stock up on dried fruit and cereal. The rice paper was tucked between information on a course in crystals and a re-birthing weekend.

Hatha Yoga
re-energise in a gentle atmosphere
day and evening classes for beginners
pregnancy course on Wednesday mornings
ring Shanti

Libby pulled off one of the phone slips and wondered whether to try it.

The teacher's gentle voice on the phone helped her decide. 'I recommend girls start before conception, but a few sessions in these last weeks will still be good for you and the baby. We meet at the Anglican church hall. Come along just before nine thirty. Oh, and wear loose clothes.'

'Do I need to bring anything?'

'Just a towel or blanket to lie on. It's a lovely group, so don't be nervous.'

**

127

Libby arrived early. There were already a few women lying on the floor with bellies up and eyes closed. She unrolled her blanket beside the youngest looking girl and took off her shoes. Her neighbour sat up and smiled.

'Hi, I'm Judy,' she said. 'Hey, I love your leggings.'

Libby looked down. She'd appliquéd fishbones and sea snakes onto this pair. 'Thanks,' she murmured.

'They look really comfortable. Where'd you buy them?'

'I, umm, made them.'

'Really? I wish I could sew.'

'The stitches aren't very neat if you look closely.'

'You can't tell from here.'

Libby tried to change the topic. 'I've never been to yoga before,' she gabbled nervously.

'It's great. You'll enjoy it.'

Shanti came in carrying a cassette recorder and flowers. She folded her hands into *namaste* and bowed. 'Welcome,' she said as two latecomers waddled in. The women who were lying down rolled over and sat up. One was enormous.

'Chelsea's ready to drop,' Judy whispered.

'Still here, Chels,' someone else observed.

'Three days overdue and going strong,' Chelsea moaned. 'My mother-in-law's flown in to mind Timmy, so I had to get out of the house. She's driving me mad!'

The class began with breathing exercises, then massage work in pairs. Libby teamed up with Judy for the scalp and shoulder massage. 'That feels wonderful,' Libby groaned.

After the massage, they bent and stretched into complicated poses. 'Listen to your body,' the teacher kept reminding them. 'This shouldn't hurt.'

Libby puffed through the activities and wondered why holding stretches was so exhausting. Her *Waiting for Baby* book reckoned her lung capacity was over half its usual volume, yet she still felt breathless. After the last exercise the teacher led them in a chant. Libby felt odd as everyone around her began humming *Om*. After a few rounds, she mumbled along, trying not to feel self-conscious. Then they lay on their mats for relaxation. 'This is the best part,' Judy said.

At first Libby found it hard to let go, but as the teacher showed them how to focus their breath, Libby tuned in to the thrumming music and was able to drift away. When Shanti rang a bell to end the session, she didn't want to move.

'How'd you like it?' Judy asked.

Libby smiled. 'Great,' she said. 'I feel all floaty.'

'It's good isn't it?'

'Who's coming to the café?' a tall woman interrupted.

'Me,' Chelsea shouted. 'This might be my last chance.'

'You said that last week!'

Judy rolled up her mat and talked Libby into joining them for coffee. A few women had to pick up kids or go to appointments, but most of them lumbered across the road to a café and flopped into comfortable cane chairs. 'This is Libby,' Judy said, introducing her to the others.

'I like your leggings,' Chelsea told her. 'All my maternity stuff is so boring.'

'She made them,' Judy said.

'Do you take commissions?'

Libby shook her head. 'The sewing's really messy ...'

'I reckon something like that would sell for fifty dollars.'

'Fifty dollars?' Libby looked at her leggings. 'They only took a few hours to make.'

'For fifty dollars, I'd buy a pair.'

'What other designs do you do?'

'Mainly ocean themes, but I guess I could do anything.'

'How about zodiac signs?' Libby nodded, but then the coffees arrived, and they started talking about episiotomies.

Tran almost wet herself when she heard about the Buddhism lessons. 'Why don't you come over and talk to Grandma? You won't have to pay her to ramble on about the Scriptures. She'd talk all afternoon. For free.'

'They teach you meditation.'

'And chanting.'

'No more,' Tran said, covering her ears. 'I'll come to the aromatherapy class, but there's no way I want to spend Saturday afternoon chanting. It's like you said, Beth, you don't have to go to church to believe in God. Same goes for Buddhism.'

**

The aromatherapy lesson was great. 'Essential oils contain the life force of a plant,' the teacher began. She went on to tell them how the use of herbs, oils and incense has been traced back to the Egyptians in 1500 BC. After explaining the medicinal history, she showed a chart of the human olfactory system.

'Oh no,' Ashleigh moaned. 'I thought I'd finished biology for the year.' Thankfully the teacher kept it brief. Then came the fun part. With a partner they had to guess the names of five essential oils. Lavender and tea-tree were easy. So was peppermint, but only Tran was able to guess camphor. She said her grandmother kept sachets of it in her cupboard. Beth really liked the last one, geranium. The teacher put a few drops of lavender into a carrier oil and showed them how to give each other a face massage. Britt was Beth's partner.

'Forget uni,' Beth told her. 'You should do this for a living.' Britt smiled and pinched her ear.

'Thank you for coming,' the teacher told them at the end of the class. 'Next week we'll be working with oils that invigorate the body and give your mind clarity. Some of you may find that helpful over the festive season.'

'We should have done this before the exams,' Ashleigh muttered. 'I could have used some mind clarity.'

'If anyone wants to mix their own blend,' the teacher continued, 'I have time before my next session. You can match oils with your personality traits to create a signature blend.'

'Just like Elizabeth Taylor or Priscilla Presley,' Britt whispered. 'How much does it cost?' she asked.

'It varies,' the teacher replied. 'There's a price list on the wall.' They listened as the teacher built up a profile of another student who had stayed behind. Once she had a case history she chose a few drops of different oils to add to a bottle of jojoba or almond oil.

'Shall we have a go?' Tran asked.

'It's pretty expensive.'

'Her oils are cheaper than the ones at the chemist. They're probably better quality too.'

'I've only got ten dollars with me,' Beth said.

Tran checked her wallet. 'I can lend you a couple.'

They filled in the medical history forms. Beth paused

at the 'recent operations' question, then firmly ticked 'No'. When they'd marked all the boxes they had to choose whether they wanted oil for relaxation, de-stressing, mind clarification or stimulation. They decided to choose a different one each. 'I bags stimulation,' Britt laughed.

'I need de-stressing,' Ashleigh said, 'so I'll take that.'

'Do you want relaxation or mind clarification?' Tran asked Beth.

'Relaxation.'

'That leaves me to be the brilliant one.'

'You can share my stimulation mixture before Jack's party,' Britt offered.

'Thanks!'

The teacher came over to work with them as a group. 'You're going to try one of each are you?'

'That way we can share,' Ashleigh explained. They read the list of oils then picked up the bottles and started sniffing. Tran chose a herb combination. Ashleigh settled on chamomile, bergamot and a lemony one called Melissa, and Britt's uplifting blend smelled like some yummy dessert. She rubbed a few drops onto her wrist while Beth tossed up between rose or rosewood.

'The rosewood smells like air freshener,' Britt said, wrinkling her nose, so Beth chose rose. They paid the teacher and took an information sheet telling them what the full course offered.

'What do you think?' Ashleigh asked as they walked into the city.

'It was fun.'

'Will you go back next week?'

'I'd love to do the whole course,' Britt said, 'but

buying the oils is too expensive. I'll use my blend for a while and see if I feel more stimulated.'

'I think she meant stimulated as in uplifted,' Beth said.

'No, uplifted is how she'll be feeling after next week's introduction to Buddhism,' Tran said laughing.

Libby: 33 weeks

'Do you want to watch the birth?'

'Do you want me to?'

'I asked first,' Libby snapped. 'You only need to say yes or no.' Darren sighed. He wanted to tell her that pregnant women were meant to bloom, not turn into sarcastic shrews, but he didn't want to start another fight. Maybe it was her hormones again.

'If you want me to be there, I will, but I'm not much good around blood and stuff like that.' He hesitated. 'I want to be nearby though. You know, in the corridor or waiting room.'

Libby smiled. She liked it when he was honest. 'That's cool. Ashleigh's hanging out to be the one to hold my hand and perve. As long as you're in yelling distance!' She put her head on his chest. 'Can I have a cuddle?'

Darren stroked Libby's hair. As he hugged her he felt something kick. 'Hey, was that the kid?'

Libby nodded. 'The little ballerina has woken up.'

'Feels more like a footballer to me. Doesn't that hurt?'

She grinned. 'Not really. I quite like it. During the day anyway.' As they held hands and kissed, Libby remembered what her yoga teacher had said about enjoying each moment: *Let go of the past and the future. Concentrate on the now.*

Libby tried to fill her lower lungs with air. Then she sighed. 'Let's go over to the café for dinner,' she suggested.

'Can we afford it?' Darren asked.

'No, but we may as well splurge before we have to fork out for a baby-sitter.'

Darren took out his wallet. 'I've got seventeen dollars and sixty-five cents. How about you?'

'Twenty-one dollars and forty cents. I'm rich!'

Darren laughed. 'Looks like it'll have to be pasta if you want dessert too.'

'We could have toasted sandwiches at home, then go over for dessert.'

Darren took her hand and led her to the door. 'C'mon, let's make a night of it. If I help Dad paint the shed next weekend, he should be good for a loan.'

They chose a table by the verandah. The placemats were dotted with old stains, but there was a sprig of Geraldton wax flowers in a jar and a candle flickering from a bottle in the middle of their table. They ordered spaghetti with garlic bread and the house salad.

The restaurant was popular with students. Although it was cheap, the atmosphere was dark and cosy. Darren and Libby ate slowly and chatted about the year ahead. It was a beautiful evening. The romantic mood of the café washed over them and after polishing off two slabs of mud cake they strolled hand-in-hand beside the river. A party boat was cruising towards the Narrows Bridge. Waves of lantern light swung over the water and they could hear the guests' laughter. They paddled their toes for a while and gossiped about school friends, then they went home and snuggled in bed. It had been a perfect night, and for once Libby was too tired to dream.

Beth shoved her backpack into the boot with her friends' luggage. 'Is there room for my boogie board?'

'Yeah, put it on the roof with my board.' Beth ran back to lock the door, then climbed onto the back seat.

'So your dad was okay about you coming down?' Britt asked.

'Yeah, Ashleigh's mum rang to say they'd keep an eye on us, and Mum told him the break would take my mind off waiting for the results.'

'Don't worry,' Ashleigh said. 'Mum and Dad sleep, read the papers and go to the wineries when we're at the cottage. We'll hardly see them.'

'Mum thinks the shed is right beside the house.'

'Well, it's in the same paddock.' They laughed.

'I haven't been to Margaret River since last year,' Britt said. 'I wonder if anything's changed.'

'The beach is still the same.'

'I hope the surfies have changed. Last year's lot weren't much to look at.'

'I'll let you know. I'm going to go down early each morning for a surf, then sit under a tree and read magazines all day.'

'You'll get bored.'

'Wait and see,' Tran said, as she accelerated out of Ashleigh's driveway. 'Anyway, I'll be able to watch you and Ashleigh chanting. That should be fun.'

'How was the class?' Britt asked.

'Like being back at school,' Ashleigh groaned. 'Boring!'

'I liked it,' Beth said.

'I thought you'd had enough study for one year?'

'It was different from school. After seventeen years of worrying about purgatory and guilt it was weird to think that I might be a reincarnated frog.'

Tran laughed. 'Perhaps we were in the same pond.'

'No, I'm serious.' She thought about the spirit image of Danni which had come to her in Ashleigh's tree house. 'I thought the whole reincarnation thing was interesting.'

'You must have heard it before.'

'Mmm, but I've never really *thought* about it. All that talk about following the middle path and doing things in moderation makes sense.'

'Someone change the subject, quick,' Tran said, 'before she starts lecturing us on the Four Noble Truths.'

Britt passed round a bag of chips, then gave Beth the map. 'Here,' she said, 'you can tell Tran how to get on the South-Western Highway while we eat.'

**

'How was the trip?' Gail asked.

'Great,' Beth said, dumping her dirty washing into the laundry basket. 'I got heaps of cello practice done in the paddock behind the shed. The cows were a bit surprised but it was fun playing in an open space and it took my mind off my results.'

'Not long now till you find out. I'm sure you'll have enough to get into UWA.'

'I hope so. Actually I was thinking about you when I was down south, wondering why you never continued with your music. Grandma reckoned you had a gift for the cello as well as the piano. She said you travelled interstate to concerts and competitions.'

Gail smiled. 'Yes, I was good,' she said quietly. 'But then I met your father and we started a family.' Beth looked away. How could her mother have given up music to become a housewife? She sighed and wished her strong-minded grandma was alive. Being home was already suffocating her.

'Did you think any more about me moving in with Sally?' she asked her mother.

'Actually Auntie Carol rang while you were away. Did you know that Ruby had to go back to Kuala Lumpur?' Beth nodded. 'Poor thing,' Gail continued. 'I hope she'll be able to finish her degree over there.'

'And?' Beth interrupted. 'Did she talk to you about me moving in?'

'Mmm.'

'So what do you think?'

'I'm not sure. It would cost more,' Gail replied. 'You'd have to help out.'

'Tran reckons her second cousin needs a waitress. I was going to try out for the job anyway.'

'Wait till your dad comes home. We can talk about it after dinner.' Beth nodded and went for a walk to prepare her argument.

**

'Living near uni would be cheaper than buying me a car to commute in from the suburbs,' she told her parents after dinner.

'Good try, Princess, but who said anything about buying you a car?'

'Dad, I'll be turning eighteen soon.'

'So will lots of other kids. The buses are full of eighteen-year-olds.'

'But what about late classes? Sally reckons a lot of her tutorials are held in the evenings, so that external students can attend.' Beth paused. She knew this was her best argument. 'I don't want to catch the bus at night. There are too many sickos around.'

Jim tapped his fingers on the chair and tried to look unconvinced. 'Even if you lived near uni, you'd still have to get home ...'

'Sally's flat is so close. Heaps of people go down Stirling Highway. I'm sure someone could drop me off after class. If not, I could ride my bike.'

'And what's to stop the same sickos dragging you off your bike?' her dad asked.

Beth grinned. 'C'mon, Dad. I'd be way too fast for them!'

'In your dreams,' her brother laughed.

Beth came up with different reasons, but it was the fact that her cousin still went to mass that clinched it with her mum. Gail reckoned Sally would be a steadying influence. Beth tried not to look smug. Sally did go to church every Sunday, but the rest of the week Beth knew she liked to party. In the end they compromised. 'If you keep an eye on James while I teach Summer School, then you can move into Sally's flat on the Australia Day weekend,' her mother said.

140

Beth leapt into the air, then gave her mum a bear hug.

'And,' Gail continued, 'we'd still like you home on weekends.' Beth nodded. Baby-sitting James for a few weeks wasn't a problem. It would take that long to sort through the junk in her room. As for the weekends, she'd break away first and worry about that later.

Libby: 35 weeks

Darren and Libby agreed to spend Christmas Day apart. 'It's so stupid that we can't be together.'

'Yeah, but whose house would we go to?'

'We could start at one, then move on to the other.'

'Do you really want to have lunch with my parents?'

Libby tried to imagine the atmosphere. She'd only visited twice and that was before the Eriksons heard the news. She shook her head. 'Imagine if both our families got together for Christmas lunch. Wouldn't that be interesting?'

'Awesome. Now close your eyes and I'll give you your present.'

**

Gail loved Christmas. She was up early to peel vegies, stuff the turkey and make fruit punch. She had an ice-cream pudding in the freezer and James had decorated the table, so they were able to get to church in plenty of time.

As a Christmas gift, Gail had asked Jim and Elisabeth to be civilised, so lunch was strained but peaceful. James lightened the atmosphere with stories about his footy mates and Gail was grateful to him. Libby and Jim were polite but avoided being alone together. Gail knew it was hard for Jim to sit beside Libby in full bloom, but she also sympathised with her daughter. She remembered her first pregnancy and how hot she'd felt during summer.

Jim fell asleep after lunch and James went to test his new computer game, so Gail and Libby took their coffee into the garden.

'Would you like me to come with you when you go into hospital?' Gail asked, as they sat beneath the lemon-scented gums. Libby almost choked on her coffee. Her mum laughed and patted her back. 'The idea's not so terrible is it?' she teased.

'No,' Libby spluttered. 'I'm just surprised.'

'If you'll let me, I'd like to help.'

'Thanks, Mum,' Libby said. 'But Darren said he'll be there. Ashleigh's begging me to let her come too, but I'm not sure. They don't always get on.'

'Do what's best for you, Libby. As long as you have someone you trust …'

'Are you upset that it won't be you?'

Gail squeezed Libby's hand. 'Whatever's best for you,' she repeated. 'There's something else,' Gail continued. 'Don't get angry … but I just want to make sure you've considered all the options.' Libby looked away. '*If* you gave up the baby,' Gail continued, 'and you wanted to keep in touch, it might be possible. Adoption laws are more relaxed now. Kids are encouraged to find their birth mothers. There are so many infertile couples desperate for babies, they may even let you visit regularly. I saw a show on TV where that happened. I think it was in Victoria. But of course that's only if you *wanted* to see the baby.'

It was Christmas Day so Libby tried not to snap.

143

'Thanks, Mum,' she said. 'But I have thought about the other options. I've spent hours thinking about other options. Something inside ends up telling me I should keep it.'

Gail drained her coffee and wondered what else she could say. Libby sipped quietly. She knew her mum was making sense. Having a baby would be more than playing dolly dress-ups. Real babies peed and vomited and screamed for hours. Was it just pride, she wondered. Her mum had left yesterday's newspaper open at a page with statistics on juvenile crime. Most offenders came from single parent families.

'The criteria for parents is strict,' Gail tried again. 'They're screened really carefully.'

Libby knew things between her and Darren were shaky. He was trying really hard, but she couldn't squash the feeling that in the end it would be just her and the baby. Would their kid resent not having a dad if Darren decided he couldn't hack it? 'I'll think about it,' she murmured, then regretted the words as she saw her mother's smile of relief.

**

Libby and Darren brought home leftovers, so in the evening they picnicked on their balcony and shared stories about their families. 'What a still night,' Darren muttered between mouthfuls of turkey.

'Let's go for a walk,' Libby suggested.

'Good idea. I might be able to make room for pudding.' They strolled arm in arm, listening to the lapping water. Parrots and lorikeets were squawking over night lodgings and the fat cotton palms stood beside the path like sentinels.

'I wonder what we'll be doing next Christmas,' Libby whispered. Darren put his arm around her shoulders and said nothing.

Perth sweltered through a heatwave as Beth counted the days until she could ring and find out her results. She went to bed early the day before they were posted, but barely slept during the humid night. In the morning, Gail knocked on Beth's door and put a glass of iced water on her bedside table. 'I'm off now, darling,' she said. 'Good luck with your phone call. The lines should be free soon. Ring during my break to let me know your score.'

Beth blinked and stretched her arms. 'What time is it?'

'Just after eight.'

'Where's James?'

'He's already at the computer. Make sure he has a break sometimes.'

'Okay. Have a good morning. I'll call you later.'

Beth rubbed the ice along her arms and stared out the window. The pumpkin vine in the vegie patch was already wilting. It looked like being another scorcher. She got up, put her student number, PIN and a sheet of paper by the phone and dialled the results information line. The number was engaged, so she made herself a coffee, then tried again. A recorded voice greeted her and asked whether she would accept the call charges. Beth pressed 0 and the voice began reciting main menu options.

Beth took a deep breath, chose subject results and

entered her student number and PIN. After all the hours of study and worry, hearing her results from a machine seemed bizarre. As the voice spoke, she scribbled scores onto the paper. English was good. Maths was okay. What about music?

'C'mon,' Beth muttered, then the voice droned, *Music: 84 per cent.* Excellent! She'd passed. Beth held her breath as she waited to hear her scaled tertiary entrance score. 81 per cent. Yes! She pressed the main menu button to find out if 81 per cent was enough to get into her first choice. It was. Beth kissed the phone. 'I've done it!' she yelled. If they liked her audition, she'd soon be studying music at UWA. It was a big 'if', and she'd have to wait a few weeks to find out, but at least her marks made her eligible.

'Are you okay?' James yelled from his room. Beth danced in and kissed him.

'I passed everything,' Beth said.

'Good one,' James muttered as he wiped his cheek. 'But save the mushy stuff for Mum.'

'I've passed!' she yelled again. The neighbour's dog howled as Beth laughed and ran to call Ashleigh. 'Come on, come on,' she muttered as the phone brringed. 'I passed history!' she screeched.

'Is that you, Beth?' Ashleigh's dad asked.

'Oh, sorry, Mr Lewis. Is Ashleigh there?'

'I'll go and see. She set the alarm for five o'clock so she could ring up for her results. I think she's gone back to sleep now. Oh, hang on, someone's just turned on the shower. Do you want me to get Ashleigh to call you back?'

'Umm, can you ask her to meet me at the park? Tell her I'll leave in fifteen minutes.'

'Righteo. Oh, and congratulations, Beth.'

'Thanks, Mr Lewis. See you.' Beth drained her coffee and gobbled some toast. Then she brushed her teeth and pulled on shorts and a top. 'I'll be back in half an hour,' she called to James.

'Mmhmm,' he mumbled.

**

Beth waved as Ashleigh pedalled towards her. 'How did you go?'

'What?'

'How did you go?'

Ashleigh skidded to a stop and dropped the bike. 'I passed. I got 86 in politics, 76 in literature and 79 in English!'

'How about biology?'

'That was my worst. Only 63 per cent, and I thought I'd done well on that exam. But I can't believe the politics score. How about you? Dad said you passed history.'

'Yep, scraped through with 61 per cent, but I did really well in English and music. Maths was pretty average, but my graded score was 81 per cent, enough to get into music.'

'Have you spoken to the others?'

Beth shook her head. 'Let's go and call them.'

'Where are we going to celebrate?'

'Didn't Britt say something about that new nightclub? Jupiters, or whatever it's called.'

Beth frowned. 'It's all right for you, but I haven't got any ID.'

'If I show mine, they won't ask you.'

148

'Yeah, sure. I always get asked.'

'Well what about the Pizza Pit?'

'Yeah, that'd be better. Then we can go to the beach afterwards. It's almost a full moon.'

'Let's hope Tran did well. She reckons her parents have agreed to a pool party for New Year's if she passes everything.'

'Well hurry up and grab your bike. We can call her from my place.'

Libby: 37 weeks

A forty-degree stinker was forecast. Libby walked around the unit in a sarong and an old singlet of Darren's. It was midday. She hadn't brushed her teeth and her hair was lanky. She looked dreadful and hated whoever said that women blossomed during pregnancy. 'Probably a man,' she snorted.

In contrast to the size of her belly, the part of her that was once *Libby* was wilting. Shrivelling. Crumbling into an automaton called *mother*. The community nurse smiled and said she ought to get as much sleep as she could before baby arrived, but every night Libby woke up groaning with leg cramps. Blue veins meandered over her cow-breasts like smelly cheese and her back ached constantly. Being pregnant sucks, she thought.

Darren was patient with her moods most of the time, but when the whingeing became too much, he spent the day surfing with his mates. Despite living in a block of flats, Libby felt isolated. Ashleigh had gone south for a family holiday, and she hadn't seen Britt and Tran since they'd celebrated passing their exams. She was sick of embroidering ducks and she was too big to play her cello. Some days it was hard not to be depressed.

When she felt really down, Libby caught the bus to the top end of Kings Park. Her favourite place was near an enormous gum tree, just back from the intersection.

Libby called it the cockatoo tree, because every summer a mob of visiting Major Mitchells used it as a meeting place. Each day they gathered to swoop and flutter and mate.

Libby liked to sit on a rug in the shade, watching the birds, traffic and joggers. She felt peaceful, in limbo. Sometimes she sat there for hours, basking in the warm eucalyptus smell of the bush. Then, if it wasn't too hot, Libby walked home along the cycle paths that meandered through the park.

She felt the first Braxton Hicks 'rehearsal' contraction while she was daydreaming under the cockatoo tree. She'd been thinking about her grandma, remembering the last family Christmas at her grandparents' house, when the pain hit. She was glad she'd read about the practice contractions in her *Waiting for Baby* book, otherwise she might have panicked. As it was, she sat quietly and rubbed her tummy until the period-like pain had passed.

Darren was reading a course outline when Libby came home. 'Hi,' she said, bending to kiss him. Darren reached out to hold her, but Libby wriggled free. 'I'll be back in a few minutes,' she said. 'I have to do something.'

Darren followed her into the bedroom and watched her sort through their drawers. She packed some undies and a nightie, then waddled into the bathroom. 'What're you doing?' he asked. 'Moving out?'

'No such luck. It's my hospital bag.'

'You're not due for three weeks.'

'Yeah, but my book says it's good to be organised ahead of time. I had my first Braxton Hicks while I was at the park.'

'Your first what?'

Libby showed him the page in her book. Darren read it, then reached out to hold her again. 'So, it's really going to happen,' he murmured.

Libby closed the book and leant against him. 'It's gotta get out somehow,' she sighed.

'Are you sure you want to give away *all* your old toys and books?' Gail asked.

'I won't be playing with them at uni.'

'But you might like to keep some special things, like these *Winnie-the-Pooh* books. One day you might want them,' her mum hinted.

'As if …' Beth began, then sweat broke out along her back as she remembered.

'Don't hold your breath waiting to become a grandmother,' she said quietly as she hoisted the box onto her hip.

After finishing with the toys and books, Beth began sorting through her wardrobe. She sighed. Her clothes were so boring. Out-of-date fashion statements hung alongside sensible blouses and tired jeans. Beneath them, daggy shoes she hadn't put on in years stood beside her well-worn boots. Beth smiled. She loved her green boots. They were worth every dollar she'd saved for them.

Beth lay all her clothes across her bed and began making piles; a *definitely chuck out* pile, a *definitely keep* pile and a *maybe* pile. The *keep* pile was pathetically small, so Beth had another sort through the *maybe* pile. There were a few pieces that could be salvaged. Perhaps if she bought some things from the craft store she could liven them up. Make them interesting.

Beth was good at sewing. When she was little she loved making clothes for her dolls. She used to sew presents for her grandmother too: pincushions, samplers or lavender sachets – things that were easy to make, but which her grandmother treasured and kept in her bedside drawer.

Beth kissed the faded photo of her grandma, tossed the rejected *maybes* into the *definitely chuck* pile and shoved it all into a rubbish bag. Then she tied the bag onto her bike and cycled to the Salvation Army shop. After handing over her old things, she went to rummage through the other clothes.

There was a rack of sixties and seventies gear. Beth looked for outfits that she could cut up, revamp with buckles, or dip into dye. She found some faded flairs and two tops that had potential, then headed off to the craft shop.

As she locked her bike, Beth noticed a new salon across the road. She ran her fingers through her hair and checked how much money was left in her wallet. Her hair had always been long. She wondered how it would look short.

She walked over to study the photos in the window, trying to imagine the hair without the models' gorgeous bones and make-up. The hairdresser wasn't busy, so Beth went in to look through a book of styles. Then she asked how much. 'It's normally twenty-five dollars for a wash and style, but if you're a student, I could do it for twenty.'

'How about a cut and no wash?'

The hairdresser laughed. 'How much can you afford?' she asked.

'I've got twenty dollars, but I need to do some shopping.'

'I'll tell you what, we've just opened and it's quiet. I'll do it for sixteen. How about that?'

'Great,' Beth replied and sat down in the chair.

Libby: 39 weeks

Although Libby squeezed her vaginal muscles, the water kept gushing down her thighs. She crossed her legs but the puddle on the footpath grew wider. Libby tried not to panic. She wasn't due for another week. She dumped the groceries and leant against a fence, bracing herself for a contraction, but there was only a vague cramping feeling. Like another Braxton Hicks.

If her waters were breaking she needed to go to hospital. Dr Wong had warned her that once the amniotic sack broke, the baby risked infection. Libby hoisted the groceries onto her hip and tried to hurry, but the shopping slowed her down. She looked around for someone to help, and noticed the piddly line following her along the pavement. Libby burst out laughing and more water whooshed down her legs. She felt like the little piggie in the nursery rhyme, going *wee, wee, wee* all the way home.

The flow slowed to a trickle by the time Libby made it to the flat, but the cramping feelings were stronger. She dumped the groceries and rang for a taxi. 'Could you, umm, make it as soon as possible,' she told the receptionist. 'I think I've just gone into labour.'

After repeating the address, Libby put her overnight bag beside the door, watered the pot plants, and checked that the windows were locked. There was no point ringing Ashleigh. She was still in Margaret River. She wrote a note for Darren and realised that her hands were trembling. As she waited by the gate, Libby wondered whether to run back inside and ring her mum. Before she could decide, she saw a taxi tearing down the road towards her. The driver jumped out and bundled her bag into the back. Libby began telling him not to panic, and then the first real contraction squeezed her guts.

'Which hospital?'

'King Edward,' she gasped and leant back in the seat to recover.

The afternoon traffic was heavy. The driver glanced in the rear-vision mirror and told her to hang on. 'It's okay,' Libby said. 'It's only just beginning.' But the contractions felt stronger and she couldn't help gasping at the pain.

'Out of the way, idiot!' the driver shouted to a delivery van. He swung into the next lane and a truckie hit the brakes behind them, blaring his horn. Her driver gave him the fingers, put his foot down, and sped through an amber light. Two traffic lights later, he screeched into the emergency driveway. 'Quick, she's having a baby,' he called to an orderly. Libby held out some money, but the driver wouldn't take it. 'Put it in the kid's first money box,' he laughed, relieved that they'd made it in time.

The orderly helped Libby inside where she filled in some forms. Then they took her to a room to be checked internally.

'Almost four centimetres. That's good,' the nurse said, but Libby knew there were six more to go.

'Is anyone coming to help you?' another nurse asked. Libby shook her head.

'No partner or family?'

'My boyfriend might come. I left him a note,' Libby whispered between contractions. Then she realised how pathetic that sounded.

**

Darren opened the door and stepped into a puddle of defrosting peas and ice-cream.

'What the ...' Then he saw Libby's note on the table.

'Damn, it's early,' he cried, running round in circles, wondering whether Libby had taken everything she needed. He couldn't find her hospital kit, so he grabbed a shopping bag and shoved some knickers and a nightie into it.

'What else, what else,' he muttered. Nappies, of course. Darren grabbed a handful. He stood still and tried not to panic. Libby's sewing was on the chair. That reminded him of clothes. He took a few tiny singlets and a grow-suit, then raced out the door. The traffic was thick. He pulled on his helmet and wove through the idling cars towards the cycle path. 'Emergency!' he called, cycling like crazy and ringing his bell at the joggers blocking his path.

Finding Libby in the hospital took almost as long as the cycling. Darren kept giving her name and waiting while hospital staff checked their paperwork. He was finally sent to the labour ward, but then he had to begin the process all over again. At last he found her, pacing up and down a hallway puffing. The midwife holding Libby's arm beamed at him. 'Look, here he is,' she said to Libby. 'I told you he'd come.' She moved aside so Darren could take over, then left them to it.

Darren felt suddenly awkward.

'How's it going?' he asked.

'Be glad you're a man.'

Darren squeezed her arm. 'When did it start?'

'About four o'clock. I'm almost six centimetres.'

'Oh.'

'I have to get to ten.'

'Oh.'

Another contraction began and Libby started whimpering. 'I'm frightened,' she said. 'It hurts.'

Darren looked at his watch. She'd been going nearly four hours. He knew it could sometimes take a day or more. 'Hell, Libby. I'm really sorry,' he said. 'You know, about ... everything.' Libby tried to smile, then gasped as she panted through another contraction. 'What can I do to help?'

'Just be here.'

'Do you want me to ring your mum?'

'No, just, aah ... just be here.'

Darren held her arm and led her up and down the labour ward corridors until her legs started wobbling. 'I'm cold,' she complained to the chirpy midwife. She led Libby towards the delivery room.

'Let's check how you're going,' she said. The nurse warmed her hands, then felt inside. 'Seven centimetres,' she announced. 'You're doing well.'

Darren spent the next three hours massaging Libby's legs and back. His arms ached from supporting her as she shuffled around, but he welcomed the pain. It made him feel less guilty.

At last Libby collapsed onto the bed. 'I need some pethidine,' she moaned.

'You're too close to second stage. It'd make you

woozy. Try the gas instead.' The midwife showed Libby how to gulp three deep breaths of oxygen, then drop the mask and go into quick breathing while the contractions peaked. That helped for a while, but just before midnight Libby lost it. One minute she was swearing and then she was crying. 'I can't do it,' she moaned.

'Help her focus on her breathing,' the midwife told Darren, but when he tried to, she told him to get stuffed.

'Don't worry,' the nurse whispered. 'She's going into transition. Getting angry is a good sign.' Darren held Libby's hand and watched her nails draw blood. The contractions were coming almost every minute. She hardly had time to breathe before the next one gripped her. 'I have to push,' Libby screamed.

'Not yet,' the midwife warned.

'I need to push NOW!' Libby's cheeks were flushed and her eyes were lunatic bright. She began shivering, but flung off the blanket Darren offered. He wanted to run away. To be anywhere else, but Libby's fingers were a handcuff around his wrist. 'I have to push,' she screamed, trying to scramble off the bed. The midwives helped her onto the birthing stool as Dr Wong came in to see how things were going.

'She's almost at ten,' the midwife said.

The doctor read Libby's chart, then took her other hand. 'You're doing well, Libby,' she said, 'but if you push too early your cervix could swell. And that would slow things down.'

'Aaahh!' Libby yelled. The midwife prodded her again, then nodded to the doctor. 'Okay,' she said. 'You can start pushing, slowly.' Libby gasped. 'Gently does it,' the midwife murmured.

Libby grunted and gave in to the overwhelming urge to push. It felt like she was giving birth to a basketball. 'That's it, bear down,' the midwives encouraged. Darren looked on with horror. The contractions were so violent and uncontrollable that Libby's eyes were bulging. It scared him.

Libby held her breath, then pushed.

'I can see the head.'

Darren peered into the mirror positioned between Libby's legs. A patch of hair filled the space that had once been Libby's vagina.

'Look,' the nurses told Libby. 'Can you see the head?' Libby looked, then turned her head to vomit, but she was caught by the next wave of a contraction. She screamed. Darren was puffing his breath in and out beside her. He looked ridiculous, but she was grateful for his help.

'Easy, easy. Remember your breathing ...' Libby gripped Darren's hand tighter.

'It's crowning. Stop pushing.'

'I can't.'

'She's going to tear.' Darren turned away as Dr Wong lifted the scissors for an episiotomy. He stroked Libby's hair out of her eyes as the doctor cut. An episiotomy was the thing she'd dreaded.

The next minutes were a blur. It looked as if the midwife slipped her hands inside Libby, but Darren wondered later if that really happened. Suddenly the head was squelching through. It was purple and covered in creamy stuff. Libby was grunting her heart out.

'Nearly there,' Darren told her.

'Okay, Libby, one more big push now. That's it, easy,

easy.' Darren watched his child's shoulders slide out of Libby's body. Then the rest of the baby followed in a great, violent slither. It looked blue, and for a moment Darren panicked, sure that there was something wrong. Then he saw the baby gasp and pucker its face in rage as another gush of water whooshed out behind it. As the midwife wrapped the baby, Darren checked its lower half.

'A girl,' he whispered. 'It's a girl, Libby.' Libby gave an exhausted smile, then lay back to rest. They placed the babe next to her breast and Libby began to cry. But they were tears of relief, and despite the pain she felt a strange, earthy pleasure. She'd given birth. She was a mother. Her eyes met Darren's, and he knew that, whatever happened, they would always share something special. This baby was a bond that would tie them forever.

Libby delivered the placenta and one of the midwives asked if she wanted to keep it. Libby looked puzzled.

'Some women like to eat it. Or plant it under a tree.'

'You're joking.' The midwife shook her head. Libby stared at the liver-coloured lump of meat. 'How gross,' she muttered, and the midwife took it away. Then she asked Darren if he wanted to cut the cord. He took one look at the pulsing cable of veins and turned pale.

As the doctor stitched her up, Libby let the nurses take the baby to be weighed. Darren watched in silence and tried to imagine the pain of someone sewing his testicles. He winced and thanked God he wasn't a woman.

PART TWO

Week 1: Libby

Daniella's floppy head and scrawny limbs terrified Libby. She looked so fragile. Libby was afraid to hold her, especially at bath time, when her pale skin was slippery. Libby's fear made her clumsy and that made her nervous, especially around the nurses, who seemed so efficient. The stark hospital room made her edgy and even the bed felt wrong. The sheets rustled when she moved. It was like sleeping in fish and chip paper.

But then her milk came in. The force of it surprised Libby but not Daniella. She latched onto her mother's nipple and sucked furiously, guzzling away any chance of mastitis. The nurses smiled. They clucked and cooed and told Libby she was doing a great job. Libby began to relax.

Daniella was enjoying a feed when her grandmother walked in. There was an embarrassed silence. Gail looked out the window while Libby rearranged her leaking breast into her nightie. 'The nurses say she's thriving.'

'Yep,' Libby replied, settling Daniella into her trolley.

'They said the birth went well …'

'They weren't the ones doing it,' Libby muttered.

Gail's eyes met her daughter's. 'Are you okay?'

Libby nodded. 'Just a bit sore.' She fiddled with the corner of Daniella's bunny-rug.

'I've brought you some roses from the garden.'

'Thanks.' Libby dusted her nose with the petals. They smelt like home. She plopped them on the bedside table and felt like crying. Again.

'Has Darren been in?'

'He just left.'

'Oh. Have you decided on a name?'

'We thought Daniella sounded good. Nice, but not too weird.'

'Daniella, mmm, that is nice.'

Beryl's tea trolley saved them from further pleasantries. 'Who wants a cuppa?' she asked.

Gail shook her head. 'No, I'll let Libby rest. I just wanted to …' The sentence trailed off in the clatter of cups.

'How many sugars was it, love?'

'None,' Libby replied.

'You sure? Y'll be needing extra energy now …'

'None,' Libby said. 'Thank you.'

Gail left as Beryl shoved and banged her trolley down the hallway. When the door was closed, Libby peered at her daughter, hoping she wouldn't wake. She needed a few moments to think. Gail's visit had made her remember home and how everything used to be.

**

'It's a girl,' Gail told Jim when she got home. 'They called her Daniella.' Her husband grunted and shut himself in the study.

Later Gail searched for the meaning of Daniella in a book of baby names. *God is my judge,* she read.

**

'Mum didn't even want to hold her,' Libby complained to Darren.

'Wasn't she asleep?'

'Yeah, but I wouldn't have minded.'

'Maybe she didn't want to wake her.'

'Or maybe she just didn't want to!'

Darren went to get a vase. It was no use talking to Libby when she was like this. As he waited for the duty nurse, he hoped her mood was due to feral hormones and not a sign of things to come.

**

Ashleigh came to visit too. She brought flowers and a card from the girls. 'Darren told us about your waters breaking,' Ashleigh laughed. 'I can't believe you just kept sloshing home with the shopping.'

'Thirty bucks worth of food! I couldn't just leave it there.'

'I wish I'd been there.' Ashleigh stuck out her belly and pretended she was carrying groceries. 'Ooh, I'm leaking,' she cried. 'Call an ambulance.'

Libby giggled then held her lower abdomen. 'Don't make me laugh. I'll pop my stitches.'

'Stitches?'

'Yeah, guess where.'

'Ouch. Was it terrible?'

Libby paused and looked at her friend. 'Not too bad,' she lied.

'I thought you were going to call me when it started.'

'There wasn't time, and anyway, you were in Margaret River.'

'But I was back by seven.'

'Ashleigh, at seven o'clock I was pacing the corridors. By then all I could think of was getting Daniella out.' She paused. 'And you know, Darren was really good. He didn't go to pieces like we thought he would.' Ashleigh smiled but wished Darren had been useless. She knew that was petty, but Libby was her best friend. She'd wanted to be the one to share the birth with her.

Ashleigh filled her in on the gossip until Libby started yawning. Then she took the hint and picked up her bag to leave. As Ashleigh stroked Daniella's blotchy cheek and hugged Libby goodbye, she sensed that everything had changed.

**

On the fifth day, Darren borrowed his dad's car and drove them home. He helped Libby unpack, then went to organise lunch. As he left the room, and Libby put their baby to her breast, Darren saw that giving birth had changed her. She was more capable, or mysterious, or something. He unwrapped the ham for their sandwiches and wondered whether becoming a father would morph him into an adult too.

Daniella sucked herself to sleep, then Libby lowered her into the pram. 'Yum,' she said as Darren handed her a sandwich. 'Just what I needed.' Darren smiled and bent to kiss Daniella's forehead. Her skin had a milky flavour and her fine white hair reminded him of photos of Scandinavian cousins he'd never met.

'Mum and Dad will want to see her,' he said. Libby kept chewing. 'Will you come with me?' Darren asked.

'Will they want me to?'

'I don't know,' Darren replied. 'They might want to

wait a few weeks.'

'Till you come to your senses and leave?'

'That's not fair!'

'You're right, I'm sorry. Of course I'll come, if that's what you want.' She licked mustard off her fingers. 'When do you want to go?'

'Would you feel up to it by the weekend?'

'I guess so. Might as well bite the bullet, but let's not stay for long, hey.'

Darren shook his head and hugged her. 'It's just so they can meet Daniella. Now that she's born, Dad's bound to thaw.'

'Don't hold your breath,' Libby muttered, thinking of her own father.

**

After their first meeting in hospital Gail stayed away. She ached to cuddle her grandchild, but visiting Libby was too hard. She didn't want to drop in at their flat. Seeing the double bed and Darren's dirty socks in the washing basket would make the situation real. So James was her messenger. He delivered casseroles to the flat and the two women met at the park instead.

Daniella was a fussy baby. Gail watched her daughter struggle to settle Daniella and forced herself not to help. 'Wouldn't you like to hold her?' Libby asked.

'She looks so cosy in her pram,' Gail said, looking away, 'better not disturb her.' Libby bit her lip and changed the subject.

That evening Gail couldn't concentrate on the movie Jim was watching. 'I'm going out to check my cuttings,' she told him.

'It's dark.'

'I'll take a torch.'

Gail sat on a bench by the shed. She shivered and watched clouds cross the moon. Ripe whiffs of the neighbour's jasmine blew into their yard, reminding her of talcum powder and Daniella. She sighed. Tonight everything reminded her of Daniella. Gail felt sorry for the wee mite. She was a gutsy little thing. And there was something else. She recognised the beginnings of love and was afraid. If Gail couldn't convince Elisabeth to give up the child, history would repeat itself, and she was willing to do anything to prevent that happening.

With no one to see her in the dark, Gail smiled. Although Daniella wore a garland of Darren's blonde hair, she knew that the baby had inherited Libby's spirit. Her funny unfocused eyes held the same intensity. Libby had been just like that as a baby.

Gail made excuses to stay away until she felt her self-control return. When they met at the park again, Daniella began fussing while Libby was at the toilet block. Gail reached into the pram and Daniella's head flopped onto her hand. Daniella sucked at the skin beside her grandmother's thumb and Gail melted.

When Libby came back, she found her mother, not Daniella, in tears. 'Why don't you hold her?' she said, and, before Gail could refuse, Libby scooped Daniella into her grandmother's arms. Daniella burped, nestled against Gail and fell asleep. That was the end of Gail's resistance. Her blood, diluted with Libby's, flowed through the baby's veins and she stopped mentioning the adoption agency.

Beth was ecstatic when she heard she'd been accepted into UWA's music program. Cello practice became a pleasure and each day she spent a few hours going over favourite pieces. She wanted to be confident when her course started.

Although Beth had to mind James every morning, her afternoons were free, so she usually went to the beach with her friends. It was a strange time. They were excited about starting uni, but knew that in a few weeks they'd be going their separate ways.

'Have you decided where we're going for your birthday?' Ashleigh asked as they cycled back from the beach one afternoon.

'I want to go to a club but can't decide which one.'

'We still haven't been to Jupiters. Why don't we go there? Spud said it was really good.'

'I want it to be just the four of us.'

'Mmm, I know. I was just telling you what Spud said.'

'All right,' Beth said, changing gear. 'Let's try Jupiters. I can't wait to walk through the door and flash my ID without stressing about being under-age.'

'Don't forget we're taking you out to dinner first.'

'Where are we going?'

'It's a secret, but you need to be ready by seven on

171

Saturday. Tran's going to pick you up after she gets me.'

'What are you wearing?'

'My black pants and white top. Have you bought anything with your mum's birthday money yet?'

'No. I thought I'd go into town tonight. Dad said he'd give me a lift. D'you want to come?'

'Okay.'

'How about we collect you at six?'

'Sounds good, see you then.' Ashleigh turned into her street and Beth pedalled the last few minutes alone.

**

Beth found a purple shift in a boutique off the mall. They were having a closing down sale, so there was enough money left over to buy matching shoes. Her dad had given Beth antique earrings for her birthday and helped James pay for a matching chain. She was amazed that her dad had chosen so well. The earrings dangled perfectly below her short hair.

'What's happened to my little princess?' he asked as Beth checked her reflection.

Beth's smile faltered, then she leant over to kiss him. 'She grew up.'

'Mmm,' Jim smiled before launching into a lecture about drink-driving and the type of men who frequent nightclubs.

'We'll be careful, and I told you before, Tran drinks mineral water when she's driving.'

'Give me a call if she changes her mind, or catch a taxi home.' He reached into his pocket for his wallet. 'Here, take this just in case.'

'Thanks, Dad.' Tran's headlights flashed in the driveway.

'Have a great time,' Gail called from the study.

'Okay. See you.' Beth grabbed her bag and ran out to greet her friends.

'Happy birthday!' they yelled.

'Dags, you know it was last Wednesday.'

'Yeah, but we're celebrating tonight. Close your eyes.'

'Why?'

'Just do as you're told.'

Beth closed her eyes and tried to guess where they were going. After a few minutes they stopped again. She was tempted to peek, but Britt was wrapping a scarf around her eyes.

They helped her out of the car, then led her along a path and across some lawn. She could smell jasmine. Her friends giggled, then she heard a male voice. Britt spun her around and took off the blindfold. 'Surprise!' they cried.

Beth opened her eyes. They were in Ashleigh's yard. Except it was decorated with fairy lights. They'd made a crepe-paper path leading to the tree house and Beth could see lanterns swinging from branches in the pepper tree.

'Good evening, madam.' Beth turned and saw Spud, dressed in a jacket and bow tie. She almost fell over. He actually looked handsome! Ashleigh was beaming proudly behind him. 'Good evening,' he repeated. 'My name's Jason and I will be your waiter tonight.'

She must have looked shocked, because in a normal voice Spud whispered, 'Don't worry, I'm only serving the food, then I'll leave you girls to get on with your secret gossip.' Beth felt guilty for that Neanderthal comment she'd made last year. Had Ashleigh told him? As 'Jason' led them to the tree house rope, she wondered how her friend had seen the treasure below his tough-boy act.

Spud helped them climb into the tree, then he passed up chilled champagne and glasses. Beth sat on the deck, remembering the day she'd come here alone. She pictured the tiny body, with its quivering heart, cradled in her imaginary hands. 'What are you looking so dreamy about?' Tran asked.

'Just remembering other times.'

'Remember when Nicola fell and broke her arm?' Ashleigh asked.

Beth nodded. 'She told her mum that I pushed her, but I was nowhere near her. She was showing off near the edge.'

Ashleigh laughed. 'She always was a dobber!'

'How come you've never invited me here?' Tran asked.

'You were at a different primary school.'

'Yeah, but what about since then? I like it up here. You can see all the way down the street, but the tree hides you from everyone else.'

Ashleigh laughed. 'You're welcome to come and spy whenever you like. Mum and Dad won't mind.'

'Look.' Beth pointed to Spud balancing a tray of soup bowls. He lay the tray across a basket and they carefully hoisted it up. Then he came back with garlic bread and quiche.

'This is great,' Beth told them between mouthfuls. 'The best birthday surprise ever. And, Ash, I don't know how you organised it, but Spud, I mean, Jason, is amazing. How did you get him to wear that suit?'

'He suggested it,' she replied sweetly.

'All right, I know you're dying to say I told you so. You may as well get it over with.'

Ashleigh grinned. 'I told you so!' Beth stared at her friend's boyfriend as he brought out dessert, and worried about her inability to judge people's characters.

Week 3: Libby

Libby looked forward to Ashleigh's visits, but they left her feeling frustrated. Something about their friendship had changed. She didn't feel that they were communicating. They talked, but not properly. Libby supposed it was her fault. It was hard to meet Daniella's needs and keep a sensible conversation going. And Ashleigh kept rabbiting on about uni. Why couldn't she understand how demanding a baby was?

Libby tried to go through the motions. She laughed when Ashleigh told her about Britt's new bloke, listened once again to how amazed Ashleigh was to have passed politics, and agreed that Ashleigh was right in choosing to study economics. Her own results had been average and, as her friend talked, Libby couldn't help being more concerned with the contents of Daniella's nappy than career choices. She slurped the last drops of her coke and wondered whether Daniella would get wind if she opened another can.

**

Ashleigh put off visiting the flat. Libby was still her best friend, but it was hard to talk to her now. They kept starting conversations but, just as the words began to flow, Daniella would cry or burp or feed or poo.

Then everything stopped until she settled again. Some days she didn't settle. Then Ashleigh sat around watching Libby try to calm her.

Ashleigh tried to understand. She even offered to help, not that she knew how to. Everyone said newborns were difficult, so it wouldn't always be this way. Daniella was sweet when she wasn't howling. She'd probably grow out of it. In the meantime though, their conversations were stilted. Libby had decided to defer, so she wasn't interested in talking about uni courses, but Ashleigh wanted to share everything. She wasn't as confident as Libby. Although she'd been accepted into her first choice, the thought of sitting in tutorials with a bunch of strangers made her nervous. She wished they could turn back the clock to the cosy times of sitting in Libby's room gossiping. She even longed for the early days at the unit, but they'd disappeared too. Now Darren lorded around the place, making her feel like an intruder. As if it was him, not her and Libby, who'd transformed the flat from a dingy apartment into a home.

Ashleigh wanted to say what she really thought about Darren, but she felt awkward. There were new rules now. Libby looked uncomfortable when they were all together, so Ashleigh learnt to time her visits for when he was out. When their paths did cross, Darren nodded coldly and Ashleigh felt like telling him to grow up. After Ashleigh left, Darren complained to Libby. 'She's wearing out her welcome isn't she? What do you two do all day? Sit around talking about me I s'pose.'

They often did, but Libby wasn't going admit it. 'As if we'd sit around talking about you all day,' she laughed. 'You've got tickets on yourself, Darren Erikson. Don't you think we've got better topics?' It annoyed her that whenever Ashleigh was around, Darren became arrogant, especially remembering that comment she'd made about Spud last year. Now Darren was becoming Neanderthal. Sometimes it was as if Libby and Daniella were his personal property. Libby wanted Ashleigh to know he wasn't always that way, but trying to explain it felt complicated. Something to do with divided loyalties, or maybe it was simply her own pride. Libby was too tired to try and understand it. She just knew that when Ashleigh and Darren were together, she felt like she was being squeezed.

Week 4: Beth

Valentine's day, and Beth didn't have a partner. Normally she wouldn't care, but she knew all the others would be taking someone to Nicola's party. Ashleigh had Spud, and Britt was deciding between Jack and Morgan. Beth wondered what Sasha and Darren would be doing. Then she shook her head. 'You're over him, remember,' she muttered, but sometimes that was easier said than done. It wasn't that she wanted him back. She just didn't want him and Sasha to be so happy.

She rang Tran to see what she was doing, then remembered Tran's cousin was visiting. 'Mum wants me to take Victor to the party. Why don't you come with us?' Tran offered. 'He's just arrived from Sydney. Dad keeps embarrassing him with photos of us in the bath together when we were five. I think he needs a break.'

'Is he cute?'

'I don't know. He's my cousin. He must be!'

'Okay, that'd be great.'

'We'll pick you up at seven.'

**

Victor was nice. He'd just been accepted into medicine at a Sydney uni. The trip over was a present from his parents for doing well. 'Want to swap parents?' Beth asked after Tran introduced them. 'Mine took me to a pizza place to celebrate finishing Year Twelve!'

'C'mon,' Tran said, grabbing her dad's car keys. 'Let's go.'

'Don't drink and drive,' Mr Nguyen called. 'And be careful you don't scratch the new car backing out.'

'Yes, Dad. We'll be fine.'

Nicola's house was pumping music. As soon as they arrived Tran went to dance. 'Want a drink?' Victor asked. Beth nodded. They grabbed a handful of chips and wandered into the kitchen.

'Hi, Beth.' Ashleigh was leaning on a bench, talking to Spud as he scoffed chips. Beth introduced Victor then wandered back to the lounge room. She was surprised when he followed. 'Are you studying next year,' he yelled, 'or have you got a job?'

'Studying,' Beth replied. 'I got into music at UWA. It was my first choice. I still can't believe it.'

'Which instrument do you play?'

'Cello, but I want to learn flute.'

'I love the flute. I learnt sax for a few years, but gave it up in Year Eleven. Took too much of my study time.'

'Sax is great, but I haven't got enough puff for it.'

'Tran said you have a nice voice.'

'Did she?'

Victor nodded. 'Why don't you sing something and show me.'

'You'd never hear me.'

'We could go into the garden ...' Beth hesitated. Victor was so smooth and sure of himself. Then she smiled. Tran was the same and she was okay. Maybe confidence ran in the family.

'Okay,' she said. 'Why not?'

As Victor put his arm around Beth's waist, she tried to pull in her tummy and ended up gasping as they stepped into the breezy night air. 'You okay?' he asked.

Beth swallowed. She dug her fingers into her palms and told herself to stop acting like a ten-year-old. 'Yep. Fine.' She cleared her throat.

'So, let's hear you sing.'

'What songs do you know?'

'Me?'

'Mmhmm, I don't like singing on my own. Do you know any duets?'

'I've got a dreadful voice.'

'I'll sing above you. How about that Mariah Carey song? You know ...' Beth hummed a few bars. Victor laughed and Beth wondered what she was doing out here with someone she barely knew. Then he smiled and she relaxed. He had a great smile. Just like Tran.

'Okay,' he said. 'You start.' Beth sang the first notes, then nodded for him to join in, but he leant over and kissed her open mouth instead.

'How does the next part go?' he asked when she pulled away.

'I'm not sure,' Beth replied.

'Perhaps like this.' He leant over and kissed her again.

Beth tensed. 'Why did you do that?' she asked.

Victor smiled. 'Because I wanted to. Isn't that okay?'

Beth frowned. 'No, I mean ... I don't know.' She looked away. 'I'm sorry, I guess that sounds stupid. It's just ... I'm not sure.'

'Hey, no worries. No need to make it into an issue. Why don't we go inside and dance for a while?'

181

Beth blinked as they returned to the kitchen fluorescents. She ignored Ashleigh's meaningful grin as Victor took her hand and led her towards the music. While they danced, she wondered what was wrong with her. Victor was gorgeous and she could tell Britt and Nicola were jealous. That strange tree house feeling washed over her. Then she thought about Darren reaching out a hand after the graduation ceremony. Beth shivered and forced herself to concentrate on the music. He'd only tried to kiss her. What was she so afraid of? She could sense Victor watching her. She looked up and he grinned, but he seemed a bit confused. Beth grinned back. Poor guy – talk about mixed messages ...

Week 5: Libby

Orientation Week was one long party. Darren and Libby hired a baby-sitter, but Daniella wasn't sleeping well, and after expressing enough milk for the evening Libby was so tired that they had to come home early.

Then Daniella developed a skin rash. Libby bought some ointment and stayed home, picking at food and doing half-hourly tiptoe checks while Darren went out alone. Each night he came home late, talking about people Libby didn't know.

Daniella usually woke them twice a night, but the record was five times. Libby was always the one who got up. She changed her, fed her, burped her, rocked her, but some nights Daniella still wouldn't settle. Darren knew he should feel grateful. Libby was doing a great job breastfeeding, so there was no pressure on him to help with bottles. But after a night of partying he didn't feel grateful. He felt claustrophobic. Sometimes he dreamt about a robed priestess (with blond hair like that Year Eleven girl, Sasha) tightening a noose around his throat. He'd wake up twitching as he fell into a dark hole. It didn't take a psychoanalyst to work that one out.

Although he was fed up, Darren wouldn't admit defeat. He found himself criticising Libby instead. 'You're training her to be dependent,' he'd mutter in the middle of the night when Libby got up to feed Daniella again. 'Why don't you just let her squawk for a while, instead of always mollycoddling her?'

'She's only five weeks old,' Libby snapped. 'Stop being so grumpy.'

'What about this controlled crying thing they talk about? Mum reckons she left me to cry and I learnt to stop bawling within a few weeks.'

'Yeah and look at you now! It takes you ages to trust anyone.' Libby regretted the words as soon as she'd said them, but she stuck her jaw out. She wouldn't apologise. Stuff him!

'Well, at least I didn't grow up spoilt and indulged,' he grunted, before rolling over and dozing off. Libby tucked Daniella into their bed and let her suck herself to sleep. Then she turned her back on Darren and dozed, too tired to feel miserable.

**

During the daytime Libby walked around like a zombie. She felt fat and flabby. Seeing girls in shorts and midriff tops depressed her. For Libby, crop tops were out of the question. Her tummy was like a potato sack and she could barely squeeze her huge breasts into any of her old shirts.

Darren's days were totally different. He was thriving. Although listening to him talk about uni made her jealous, Libby couldn't help laughing at his imitations of the lecturers' quirky habits and attempts to be groovy. After a day with Daniella, she was desperate to hear about the outside world. Anything would do.

Darren enjoyed his philosophy classes the most. He bought black clothes and came home spouting words like 'existentialism' and 'slave morality'. Words that Libby had to look up in the dictionary. 'What's with all this black?' she asked one morning. 'It doesn't suit you, you know.' Darren kept lacing his boots as Libby held out a shirt she'd found at the op shop. 'Here, why don't you wear this? I've even ironed it.'

'Green doesn't suit me.'

'Of course it suits you. Your eyes are green. How can it not suit you?' She knew she was nagging, but her mouth wouldn't stop. She needed to talk. About something. Anything. She had to talk before Darren left her alone again with Daniella. 'Can't you stay home this morning? There's no one for me to talk to.'

'Talk to Daniella. I can't miss another tutorial.'

'I want to talk to you …'

'I'm late.'

'But Darren …'

'It doesn't always have to be *me* that you talk to! Why don't you join a mothers' group like everyone else does?' he snapped.

'I don't want to talk about nappies and projectile vomiting. I get enough of that at home! I want to talk about other things. I want to talk to *you*. The way we used to.'

'We talk every evening. What else is there to say?'

'But …'

'Look, can't you just drop it?' Darren yelled. 'I told you, I'm late!'

She sniffed. 'I was only trying to help. Someone needs to tell you when your shirts look ridiculous.'

'Here we go again. I wasn't talking about my shirts,

185

but before you start droning on again, I like my clothes, okay?'

'It's because of that girl in your philosophy class isn't it? The pale one we met at the library. She's always wearing black.'

'Why don't you just shut your stupid face!'

Libby could see she'd scored a point, but that wasn't much consolation as she stared at the door Darren slammed behind him. Then she heard Daniella's cry. He'd woken her. Libby looked at her watch. Daniella had only been sleeping for twenty minutes, so now her pattern would be totally stuffed. The day loomed ahead. Hours of nappies, cleaning and screaming. Libby put the kettle on and tried to block out Daniella's howling. She needed a coffee.

**

When Darren came home they fought again. Libby had kept Daniella up so that Darren could bath her, but he was late. Again.

'Doesn't your daughter mean anything to you?'

'You're being melodramatic.'

'We agreed that you'd bath her. You said you wanted to spend time with her.'

'The world won't stop turning if I miss one night!'

'Well you could have rung me. I've been waiting …'

'So this is about you, not Daniella.'

'It's about both of us …' Daniella interrupted their argument with a shrill scream and Libby shoved her at Darren. 'Here, your daughter needs her nappy changed.'

As Darren wiped banana-coloured poo from

between Daniella's legs, his parents' words spun around his mind. *How do you know it's yours? She's trapped you, hasn't she, Darren?* Around and around, the words twirled like Daniella's mobile in the breeze.

In the other room Libby had turned on the telly. It was a Friday night. Darren wondered if his mates would be down by the beach. He nuzzled Daniella's tummy and put on a fresh jumpsuit. Then he lowered her into the bassinette and stroked her hair until she fell asleep.

Libby had abandoned the quiz show and was waiting in the kitchen, ready for round two, but Darren headed for the door. 'Danni should sleep for a few hours,' he said, grabbing his jacket. 'I'll be home before nine. If you express some milk, I'll get up to her during the night.'

'You make me sound like a cow.'

'Libby, I don't want to fight. I just need some space.'

'And what about me? What if I want to go out?'

'Do you?'

'Maybe!'

He looked at her tangled hair and slovenly clothes. It was hard to believe he'd once found her attractive. 'Okay, I'll be home in an hour. That'll still be early enough for you to go out.' The door rattled behind him.

'Bastard,' Libby muttered. She snibbed the lock and paced the kitchen. Then she lifted one of Darren's golf clubs and looked at his footy trophies. If she swung hard enough she might break one, but that would wake Daniella. Libby took a coke from the fridge, sculled a mouthful, then dropped to the floor. 'It's not fair,' she moaned, digging her nails into her arms to stop the tears. She thought about her family and her faith and forced herself to get up. As she wandered into the bathroom, Libby blinked at her reflection in the mirror. It was hard to believe her life had turned into this disaster. She tried to think, but it was like fighting her way out of a mist.

'Concentrate,' she told herself, but past arguments teased her. *It's all right for you, I can't just go out and forget to feed her. You're the one who wanted to have her, remember?*

Libby splashed cold water onto her face and looked up again. The fluorescent light made her look horrible. She closed her eyes, then opened them. Black spots appeared. She gripped the basin, feeling dizzy, and stared into the mirror. Then the fog cleared. Libby took a deep breath, gazed into her eyes and knew that her relationship with Darren was over. Libby didn't blame him. She was a mess. Their lives were on different tracks and she was tired of trying to bend. She would simply let go. Just like Shanti had told them at yoga.

Doing something mundane usually stopped her from thinking too much, so Libby tidied the kitchen. She scrubbed the sink and cleaned the fridge. When everything was tidy, she left a note on the bench where Darren would find it.

> *Sorry! Can I still blame it on hormones? Whatever, I'm too exhausted to go out, so I've gone to bed instead. There's a bottle of milk in the fridge. If you get up to Daniella in the night, I promise to be civilised in the morning. Thanks, L.*

**

Libby was staring at the ceiling when she heard Darren come home. There was a long silence while he read the note. Half an hour later, when he climbed into bed, Libby breathed deeply and pretended to be asleep. She knew he was getting up early to meet his dad.

After he left in the morning, Libby packed Darren's things and left his bag outside the door with another note:

> *I did a lot of thinking last night and realised that our lives are going in different directions. Thank you for helping me through the birth and these first weeks. We tried, but it hasn't worked. I'm sorry if I've been a bitch. When you've had time to think, I'm sure you'll agree that this is the best way. Ring me in a few weeks if you want to arrange visits, otherwise let's just call it quits. Good luck with uni and everything. I hope it works out well for you.*
> *Libby*

**

In the evening she heard Darren stop outside the door. Libby held her breath, hoping he'd knock, hoping that he cared enough to convince her to try again. Although she dreaded a confrontation Libby wanted *him* to make the final decision. That way she couldn't be wrong. If he knocked Libby knew she'd fall into his arms. Perhaps they could find a way to get through it. But Darren didn't knock. Libby listened as he lifted his bags and walked away. Then she started crying again.

Beth settled into Sally's flat the week before uni started. Her room was small, but it opened onto a narrow verandah. In the evenings she played her cello, met friends and watched boats cruise along the Swan. During the days she went for walks and explored the riverside suburb. The streets were a strange mixture of mansions and architecturally challenged flats. Beth liked wandering along the grassy foreshore watching pelicans make clumsy landings and listening to the clink of yacht rigging. At peak hour, joy flights jostled for air space with traffic reporters in light planes. It was a bustling suburb, totally different from the quiet neighbourhood she'd grown up in.

Suddenly it was Orientation Week. The first days at uni were a whirl of parties, meetings and information. Beth felt nervous sitting in the courtyard or cafeteria on her own. Although she forced herself to look confident and chat with other students, she wished Ashleigh was studying at UWA. Or Britt. Or Tran. But they'd been accepted into other universities. Once Beth saw Darren in the distance, but she didn't call out to him.

She met a girl called Jacinta at a lunchtime O-Week concert. They were both sitting alone. Jacinta spilt her milkshake over Beth's jeans as she tried to squeeze past her. 'Oh, I'm sorry,' she cried, trying to mop chocolate froth off Beth's legs.

'That's okay.' Beth headed for the washroom while Jacinta followed, dabbing at her legs with tissues. 'It's okay, really.' Beth unzipped her jeans and rinsed them under the tap. 'At least they'll be cool. I was boiling out there.'

'Me too. Hey, aren't you doing music history?' Beth nodded. 'We're in the same class. On Wednesday mornings. You were wearing bright leggings the other day.'

'That's right.'

'I love those pants. Where did you get them?'

'I made them during the holidays. I like sewing.'

'Wish I could do something like that. Sewing on buttons is the most I can manage.'

'What did you think of the concert?'

'I liked the girl on the harp.'

'Are you majoring in music?'

'No, music is an elective,' Jacinta replied. 'I'm doing politics. Music balances the boring subjects. I played flute in high school but I'm not good enough to make music a career or anything. How about you?'

'I'm doing music full time. I've been learning cello for six years and now I'm starting flute. Maybe we'll have the same tutor.' Beth shook the excess water off her jeans. 'There, that should do it.'

'I hope it won't stain. Can I buy you a sandwich to make up for it?'

'I've already eaten,' Beth said, 'but that milkshake looked pretty good. Do you want to share another one?'

**

191

When she wasn't busy, Beth's mind wandered back to Victor. They'd spent the rest of the evening dancing inside with the others and, although she'd enjoyed his attention, Beth avoided being alone with him again. Then she was disappointed that he hadn't tried to get her alone.

Victor kissed her cheek when Tran dropped her home, thanked her for a nice evening and said to call if she had any free time. Beth lay awake going over the evening in her head and trying to understand her feelings. Victor was a nice guy, but she didn't want to get involved. It felt too complicated. Besides, she suspected he was being polite. She didn't call, and at the end of the week Victor flew back to Sydney to become a doctor.

**

Sally's unit was a welcome haven. After her classes and music practice, Beth liked to wander down to the pier at the end of their street. She dangled her legs over the wooden boards and watched speckled jellyfish drift under the bobbing yachts. On still afternoons there were thousands of the creatures. Pee-wee clumps of tentacles swam alongside their balloon-sized parents. Each translucent body was like an umbrella-shaped heart, beating in and out as fuzzy tentacle clumps trailed along behind. The small ones reminded her of that other little heart.

Although she was happy at the flat, Beth honoured the deal with her parents and went home one night each weekend. She enjoyed her mum's cooking and it was good to be pampered. Even James was nice to her. He missed having her around, not that he'd ever admit it.

When Sally stayed over at her boyfriend's place, Beth had the unit to herself. On those nights Ashleigh or Jacinta often came over to share takeaway dinners. One night Jacinta rang to ask if she could drop by. Beth looked at her watch. It was after ten. 'Sure. Is everything okay?'

'Not really. I know it's late, but I need to talk ...'

'Of course. Come over. I'll put the kettle on.'

When she arrived Beth could see that Jacinta had been crying. She made a plunger of coffee and took it onto the verandah. 'What's wrong?' Beth asked.

'My mother rang,' Jacinta whispered. Beth pushed down the plunger and poured coffee into their mugs. Jacinta was from a town in the Wheatbelt. Beth tried to remember what she knew about her mum.

'Is something wrong with the farm?'

Jacinta stared at her. 'No, not that mother. My other mother. My birth mother. Oh, sorry, I haven't told you. I was adopted.' Beth gulped her coffee. How come, of all the people she could have met at uni, her new best friend was someone who'd been given up by her mother? Was this some kind of message?

'I knew she might call one day,' Jacinta continued. 'Jigsaw contacted me a few months ago, asking if I was willing to release my phone number. I spoke to Mum, my adopted mum that is, and then decided that if my birth mother wanted to make contact, then maybe I should let her. I told Jigsaw, but nothing happened. I was disappointed, but also relieved that she'd chickened out.'

'And now she has called ...'

'Mmhmm. This evening. I was so calm on the phone.

It was like a dream. But afterwards I freaked out. I've been staring at the wall for the last hour, wondering whether I really do want to see her. I mean ... why should I? I don't owe her anything. Mum and Dad brought me up, but then she *is* my mother. We share the same genes. It'd be nice to see if I look like her.' Jacinta picked up her mug. 'Sorry, I know I'm rambling, but I needed to talk to someone. I don't want to tell Mum and Dad that she called. Not yet. And my friends in Wagin love Mum, so they'd be biased. I hope you don't mind ...'

'No, I'm glad you told me. It's nice that you trust me that much.' Beth hesitated. 'Seeing as we're telling secrets, I have one too.'

Jacinta looked up. 'Last year, I ... umm, I had an abortion. Afterwards I kept wondering whether I'd done the right thing. Whether I'd been selfish not going through with the pregnancy. They reckon there's a long waiting list of parents trying to adopt children, but I didn't think it was right to bring an unwanted child into the world. Oh, sorry, I didn't mean it like that ...'

'It's okay. I often wondered the same thing. I'm lucky, my adopted parents are great, but given the choice I wouldn't grow up as an only child in the Wheatbelt. It was too isolated and farmers are so undervalued. Then there's the weather ...' She sighed. 'Do you know, when I was ten, I went through a really difficult time. I kept waking up in the night thinking that my mother was calling me. I felt so alone. Like I didn't have any roots. I was worried that I'd never fit in anywhere. Poor Mum used to find me sobbing. It tore her apart, and yet I love Mum and Dad. You couldn't wish for better parents.'

'It's really strange the way things work,' Beth said. 'I

was sure I'd done the right thing, but now here you are. What if your birth mother had terminated you?'

Jacinta laughed. 'I would never have known. My soul or whatever would have come down to another child I guess.' She reached out to touch Beth's hand. 'If it's any consolation, I'd have done the same thing, even though I wouldn't be here if my birth mother had made that choice.'

Beth smiled. 'Tell me about the phone call,' she said. 'What did she say?'

'It took a moment for her to say anything. I thought it was a crank caller, but then she asked if I was Jacinta Turner. I said, "Yes", then she said, "My name is Jenny. I'm your birth mother." I didn't say anything, so she told me how relieved she was that I let Jigsaw pass on my phone number. She said she'd been thinking about me for years, that she wanted to call as soon as she got my number, but that she was too scared.'

'Why was she scared?'

'She didn't say. Maybe she thought I'd hang up.'

'Are you going to meet her?'

'I don't know. She wants to, but I said I needed time to think about it.'

'What have you got to lose?'

'Everything! My identity, peace of mind. I don't want to remember those feelings I had when I was ten. That's all behind me now. Why dredge it up?'

'You must be curious …'

'Of course, but I don't know if seeing her is worth the upheaval.'

'What about your birth father?'

'She didn't mention him. Maybe he doesn't know about me.'

Beth thought about Darren. Even if he'd supported her through the pregnancy, if she'd given up their baby, how long would he have wondered about their child? Perhaps he'd be curious from time to time, but she didn't think he'd grieve for seventeen years. Not like a mother. 'Want some more coffee?'

'Yeah, thanks.'

They talked about childhood, about mothers and daughters, about men and relationships. When the café across the road closed Beth looked at her watch. It was past midnight. 'Why don't you sleep here tonight? Sally's staying at her boyfriend's. I'm sure she wouldn't mind if you slept on her bed.'

'That'd be great.'

'If you need anything, give me a yell.'

'Okay,' Jacinta said, 'and, Beth, thanks. I really appreciate it.' Beth hugged her and went to bed. She felt exhausted. Despite the coffee, she began drifting into sleep as soon as her head touched the pillow. Sometime before dawn Beth woke. She thought she heard muffled sobbing, but then she fell asleep again, and in the morning she wondered whether she'd dreamt it.

'Did you sleep okay?' she asked.

Jacinta nodded but she looked pale. 'I've decided to meet her,' she whispered.

'I think that's what I'd do,' Beth said. 'When will you phone?'

'Today, before I change my mind.'

'Do you want to call from here?'

'No, I'd rather be on my own. But thanks anyway. I'll let you know how it goes.'

'All right. I'd better get ready. I've got an early tutorial.'

'Okay, I'll go back to St Columba for a shower, then make the call.'

'Good luck.'

'Thanks, I'll need it.'

Week 7: Libby

Libby didn't remember much about the week Darren left. She rang her mum to say she'd be busy, then spent hours at home snivelling. One morning her old school friends came over. When she heard them tap at the door, Libby hid behind the curtains blubbering into her milk-stained tracksuit. She didn't want them to see her like this.

They kept knocking until Daniella woke up and started crying. Libby still didn't answer. In the end they went away, whispering. Libby came out of hiding and went to cuddle Daniella. She tickled her tummy and giggled, but her laughter was brittle. Then she began trembling. The unit seemed suddenly quiet. Too quiet. It frightened her. She put Daniella on her rug and ran down the steps to the road. But it was too late. Her friends had gone.

Each day was a challenge and sometimes Libby wondered if she was going mad. If she was, Daniella didn't seem to mind. She fed and grew and filled her nappies. Libby sang to her when she cried and sometimes she cried too. When she saw the ad for local mums to join a new mums' group, Libby sighed in relief.

Calling all New Mums.
How about joining us for a coffee and support

morning? The group is for newborns and their
mums, but older siblings are welcome too.
Ring Ronnie on the number below.

The group met twice a week at different members'
houses. At first Libby was surprised how old these
'new' mums were. Most had left professional jobs to
start a family and Libby felt self-conscious being so
young. The women were kind, but Libby didn't feel
that they really accepted her. The only thing they had
in common was babies. Ronnie, the group leader, was a
tutor at uni and she seemed especially distant. Being
around her made Libby feel like she was back at school.

'Maybe we could hold the next get-together at your
place,' Ronnie suggested one morning.

'It's too small.'

'Where do you live?'

'Towards the end of Broadway.'

'I thought it was all units down there.'

'It is.'

'Oh!' The woman's mouth sprang like a trap around
the word. She looked away wondering what to say.
Then she noticed her son eating sand. 'Oh, Joshie, don't
do that,' she called, and quickly escaped. Libby held
her head high but inside she was burning. Across the
room the other mums were drinking coffee and flicking
through magazines.

'Hey, listen to this,' Jacquie said, reading from a well-
thumbed article about stealing. 'The woman expressed
no regret and said that she would do the same again to
protect her child.'

'It's true, don't you think?' Irene added. 'I'd do
anything for my boys.'

'Not break the law though?'

'It goes on to say, *a parent's love is unconditional.*'

'That's true! I'm just starting to appreciate my own parents since having kids …'

'My dad's isn't,' Libby interrupted. They turned to stare at her. 'Sorry,' she added, 'but I think that's rubbish! About the unconditional love, I mean …' No one said anything. Even the babies seemed quiet. For a nanosecond no one kicked, gurgled, dribbled or spat. There was silence. Then the older kids started squealing again. As the group leader changed the topic, Libby felt an invisible desert surrounding her. She was drowning in politely shifting sand. She rinsed her cup and lifted Daniella into her pram. 'Anyway, I guess I should get going. Thanks for the coffee.'

The older mothers said they'd see her next week and smiled what seemed to be fake smiles. As she closed the door Libby saw the first eyebrow raise and knew she wouldn't be back. What did they know about unconditional love, she thought, striding past their architecturally designed townhouses to the bus stop. It was all very well for love to be unconditional when you had the luxury of being provided for. It was probably fun to plan after-work surprises when your husband had a secure job. The group leader's face came to mind. Even if her husband was retrenched, Ronnie had the qualifications to re-enter her field whenever she liked.

Libby hurtled the pram over the tree-cracked footpath, determined not to cry. She imagined the others discussing her. Like sharks in a feeding frenzy. Yet until ten months ago she'd planned to become just like them. She understood them. Their values were hers. If she'd chosen differently, she could have been their mirror image one day. Successful, complacent, with a doting hubby. The uneven footpath and jerky bouncing woke Daniella. She started crying.

'Oh don't you start!' Libby snapped and was immediately sorry. Perhaps her mother had been right. Maybe she should have given up Daniella for adoption. An older couple could give her so much more. Not just the fancy clothes and toys, but emotional stability as well. Libby sat down to wait for the bus and refused to give in to the tears.

**

It took James a few days to decide whether to tell his parents that Darren had gone. He didn't want to blab – Libby had told him in confidence – but seeing how strange she was worried him.

'She's gone really weird,' he said to his mum at last. 'I think she's losing the plot.'

'When did he leave?'

James shrugged. 'Last weekend I think.'

'Is she all right?'

'Not really. I don't know, she just seems strange.'

Gail put some fruit and leftover apple crumble into her basket and drove over. She could hear Daniella whimpering as she knocked at the door, but there was no answer. Gail tried the handle. It was open, so she let herself in. The place was a mess. 'Hello,' she called.

'Hang on,' Libby yelled before emerging from the bedroom with a bare-bottomed Daniella across her shoulder. 'I'm trying to change her nappy but she won't stop squealing and kicking.'

'Here,' Gail said, taking her grand daughter. 'Why don't you pop the kettle on and I'll have a go.' Libby gave in without protest, but before she turned away Gail could see she'd been crying.

'James said Darren's left.'

'Mmm, I thought you'd be happy about that.'

'Where do you keep the nappy rash cream?' Gail asked, ignoring the sarcasm.

'I ran out.'

'Her bottom's really red. Do you have anything else? Powder or vaseline?'

'There might be something in the bathroom cupboard.'

'Libby, I'm not happy that Darren left,' Gail said as she searched through the cupboard. 'I know you were both trying hard to make it work.' She paused. 'Do you think he'll be back?'

Libby shook her head and blinked back the tears, angry at the hormones that still made her emotional. 'It wasn't working,' she admitted to her mum. 'I think we both knew it wouldn't.' She bit her lip, determined not to cry. 'It's probably the best thing for everyone that he's gone.'

Gail fastened the nappy and swung Daniella into the air. 'Why don't you come back home for a few days?'

Libby shook her head. She could see how hard this was for her mum. 'No, I don't think that would be a good idea.' She tried to sound gracious. 'It's just that I get so exhausted.' Libby's voice cracked. 'Daniella needs all my attention. I don't know if I can do it much longer ...'

'I could help you if you were at home,' Gail whispered.

'But I've just settled in. If I moved back it would be admitting defeat.'

'It wouldn't have to be forever …'

Libby glared at her mother. 'You don't think I can cope, do you?'

'I do, it's just that …'

'I don't want to hear any more. I can't think straight when you start lecturing me. The door's open. Please go!'

'Darling …'

'Get out!' Libby screamed. She knocked over a saucer as she stood up. Teacups clattered to the floor and Daniella started crying.

'Libby.'

'Go!' Libby snatched up Daniella and ran into the bedroom. Gail left the fruit and pie on the bench. She hesitated at the door. Libby was sobbing in her room but Daniella's crying had stopped. She found a pen by the phone and wrote a quick note.

> *Darling, You know I'm not good at saying things, but I love you and Daniella – with all my heart. I just want you to be happy. In the beginning I did hope that you'd give her up, but now she's part of our family. I'll try and talk to your father again. Perhaps we could look after her till you're stronger … I'll come back later to check that you're okay. Be brave. I love you both. Mum*

Libby collapsed across the bed, sobbing. She took Daniella into her arms and climbed under the covers. Daniella nuzzled at her breast for a few minutes, then fell asleep. Libby stared at the ceiling and wondered if she was going mad. As she listened to her mother's footsteps going down the steps, she tried to work out why she was so angry. Perhaps her mother had scratched too close to the truth. Libby longed to admit defeat. To agree that she was too young to be a mother. That Daniella might be better off with an older couple. A normal mum and dad, perhaps even siblings.

Libby stroked her daughter's fine blond hair, and as she listened to Daniella snuffle in her sleep, she knew she could never give her up. At times like this, when she was peaceful, Libby believed Daniella was an angel from God. But why had He given her such a hard road? She closed her eyes and reached inside, trying to find her faith. Then she took three deep yoga breaths and repeated a prayer from childhood. Libby felt her mind slowly clearing as shreds of commonsense returned. 'Thank you for understanding,' she whispered. 'Please, give me patience to care for Your child.' She closed her eyes and fell asleep. When Gail tiptoed in an hour later with flowers and a fresh tub of nappy cream, she found them both sleeping peacefully, and added a PS to the bottom of her previous note:

3pm. If you need anything, please call, otherwise I'll ring you in the morning. Love and hugs, Mum

**

Daniella's crying woke Libby at dusk. She could smell the dirty nappy but wasn't ready to face it. Her head ached. She reached into the bedside drawer and took a

Panadol. Daniella nuzzled her breast, suckled for a moment, then began to cry again. Libby needed a moment to wake up so she put Daniella into her bassinette and went onto the balcony. Daniella howled.

She closed the door, but the screaming became louder. With gritted teeth Libby went inside, unwrapped the nappy and mopped up her daughter's sticky shit. The rash blooming across Daniella's fanny made her ashamed, but it was not enough to cut through her self-pity. She picked up Daniella and wondered what to do about her nappy rash. Then she saw her mother's note with the fruit and flowers and she began to cry again. Her dad was right. Mum didn't deserve this. Libby took a deep breath, then slopped baby bum cream over the red patches and fastened a new nappy. Daniella still cried, but it was more of a moan than a howl.

Libby strapped her into the travel cot and swung her back and forth. Daniella normally loved this, but tonight she just grizzled. Libby patted her back then noticed that her tapping was becoming too hard. She offered her daughter a breast. Daniella latched on and Libby thanked God that at least some part of her could offer her daughter relief. She stroked Daniella's hair. Her forehead was hot. Libby reached into the nappy bag for the thermometer and, as Daniella sucked fretfully, she stuck it under her armpit. Thirty-nine degrees! Libby told herself not to panic. Babies could have febrile convulsions if their temperature reached forty.

She sloshed cold water onto a flannel and held it over Daniella's face. Then she sponged her little arms and flushed legs. Daniella kicked and screamed but Libby ignored her protests. After five minutes of sponging she took her temperature again. Thirty-eight. 'Thank you, God,' she whispered, but Daniella was feeling less appreciative.

Libby took off her daughter's singlet and sponged her chest. Her temperature was still high. Libby rang the children's hospital. 'Keep sponging,' the receptionist said, 'and give her some Panadol. If her temperature goes higher, bring her in. Otherwise, try not to worry. You're doing the right things. Do you have a car?'

'No, but I can call a taxi,' Libby managed to croak.

'Okay, well keep calm and ring again if you need to. If her temperature rises again, call for an ambulance.'

Libby put down the phone and resoaked the flannel. Surely God wouldn't take her baby now. Not after all she'd been through. The pain of childbirth, the humiliation of her pregnancy. What would be the point in putting her through all that? She'd lost her adolescence and the pregnancy had ripped apart her family. Letting Daniella die now would be too unfair. 'Please make her better,' she whispered. 'I love her, I'll do anything ...'

As the night wore on, Libby made a swag of promises and deals with God. In the early hours of the morning, she remembered her grandma's sorrow when Grandpa died. 'God knows best,' she'd told Libby. 'He wants your pop up there beside Him and somehow we have to bear the loss.'

Libby sang lullabies as she sponged, trying to soothe Daniella. She thought about ringing her mum, but there was nothing anyone could do, and Gail would only worry. Darren? She could call him. Or Ashleigh? Ashleigh would be over in a flash. Libby reached for the phone, but as she lifted the receiver she looked at her watch. Three-fifteen. What could Ashleigh do that she wasn't already doing? Libby put down the phone. She wouldn't panic. Perhaps God was testing her. Yes, that must be it. She knew she was being irrational, but after hours of fever, nappies and diarrhoea, she didn't care.

At four-thirty Libby rested her head and dozed until Daniella started crying again. Then she ran to wet the flannel. As she lifted and patted and rocked, the sky began to lighten into a pre-dawn grey. Libby lay Daniella on the table and slid the thermometer under her armpit. Daniella squirmed. 'Stop it!' Libby yelled, not caring what the neighbours thought. 'Why can't you just shut up!'

Daniella howled and Libby sobbed. 'I'm sorry,' she crooned. 'I'm so sorry, Daniella.' Libby carried her into her bedroom, then they lay on the bed together and fell into a fitful sleep.

**

Darren sat on a bench outside the block of flats. It was only seven-thirty, but Daniella had probably been awake for hours. All he had to do was walk up to Libby's door and knock. She'd said he could have access, spend time alone with Daniella, whatever he wanted. He waited. It was his move. So why was he still sitting on the bench? If he didn't walk over now, he knew he never would.

Darren pictured Daniella's funny, unfocused eyes, her big head, chubby belly and thin kicking legs. He remembered the night she was born. How she'd slithered into the midwife's hands, and that moment when he'd looked into Libby's eyes and seen into her soul. He'd never known a moment like that. A moment without pretence. It was scary. They'd shared something big. Something that he wasn't ready for. If he walked away now, he'd be giving that up. Giving up any claim on Libby and his child. There was no halfway decision. He couldn't just see them sometimes. That wouldn't be fair on anyone.

Darren sighed. The other choice was freedom. It should be simple. Libby was offering it to him on a plate. So why wasn't he grabbing it? He thought about Libby. She was so much stronger than him. He respected and admired her, but he didn't love her. Not in a forever-after kind of way. Then he thought about Daniella. The way she gurgled into his chest. The bait was sweet, but his urge to be free was stronger. Darren took a step towards the flat, then remembered his mates at the beach and uni. 'I'm sorry, Daniella,' Darren whispered, looking up at the window. Then he walked away.

Libby had seen Darren outside the flats. Although exhausted from their sleepless night, she guessed what he was trying to decide. Strangely though, she didn't have the energy to care. Any romantic feelings for him had died. They'd drifted too far to return.

Daniella started to whimper, even though her temperature was back to normal. Libby wanted to ignore her but it was impossible. She changed Daniella's nappy, and by the time she carried her back to the window, Darren had gone. Although she'd expected it, Libby felt her chest tighten. She thought of Darren's hands stroking her hair and the smell of his chest when he pulled her close. She didn't blame him. Perhaps she'd made it too easy, but it had been her decision to have their baby, not his.

Then she thought of the slim philosophy student who liked to wear black, and something snapped. Libby crumpled onto the floor. She rocked back and forth, moaning, as tears fell onto Daniella's chubby arms. The urge to scream was overpowering, but Libby clenched her teeth. She was frightened that if she started she might never stop.

Week 8: Beth

Beth loved the location of the music department. It was tucked away in a building near the Swan River. To get there, she walked through the leafy grounds of the uni or rode her bike along the foreshore cyclepath. Most of all she loved the sound of music drifting out of the building as she approached.

At school Beth had been the choir's lead singer and one of only two cellists. Now she was surrounded by students who were passionate about their music. Their intensity encouraged Beth to push herself. She could already toot a few notes on the flute and her cello playing had improved so much that Frau Schmidt was beside herself.

One of Beth's first assignments involved teaming up with three other students to practise and perform a piece by the German composer Johann Pachelbel. Her group was assigned the *Canon in D major*. They'd all heard the piece playing in cafés and bookshops, so the first rehearsal went well. Beth plucked a baseline and lost herself in the peaceful rhythm as the violinists flew around the higher notes. Sinking into the music was like standing in summer rain. After a few sessions together their instruments blended, and Beth felt a deep sense of contentment. It was something she'd never captured playing alone.

Beth also loved her philosophy classes. Her first unit was called *Critical Thinking* and the lecturer liked to begin his tutorials with shared meditation. He reckoned it opened the mind. Once their minds were open, they were supposed to explore their beliefs and develop arguments about various issues. Bouncing ideas off other class members and watching them struggle to explain questions made Beth realise how little she knew about her own belief structure. So much had changed during the past year. She remembered the time before Darren. Then, after the termination, she'd been so determined to punish herself, until that afternoon in the tree house. Now, after talking to Jacinta, did she still think that she needed to suffer? Couldn't she become wiser without all the angst? Beth wasn't sure. On top of all that she wondered how she could blend her faith with this new Beth that was emerging?

Part of their philosophy assessment involved keeping a journal. 'Recording thoughts helps us make sense of our lives. It teaches us to question where we fit in,' their lecturer said. 'Look for patterns. Stretch your minds. Above all, learn to be honest, at least to yourself. I'll need to sight your journals, but I won't read them, unless you want me to.'

After hesitating over the first blank sheet, Beth wrote pages of questions:

Who am I?
What do I believe?
What kind of person do I want to be?
How can I learn to see through the masks people wear?

The list went on and on:

Does it matter what people think of me?
What do I value most?
Which ideals are most important to me?
What do I want in a relationship?
Is love more important than trust?

The more Beth tried to find answers, the more uncomfortable she became. Her list of questions led to more questions, but it was hard to find specific answers. Life wasn't black and white. After a while, Beth simply wrote whatever came to mind and hoped that somehow a pattern would emerge.

She also began recording her dreams. Since that night with Jacinta, Beth was having strange dreams about lost luggage and missed trains. Whenever she practised her meditation, her mind wandered to Ashleigh's tree house. She felt the sunlight warming her face and smelt the peppery leaves. It was peaceful. Too peaceful. Beth knew she had to go deeper into herself to find answers.

When her mind began looping, Beth dumped her journal and took a break with Johann Pachelbel. He couldn't help her pin down elusive thoughts, but at least his music soothed her.

Week 9: Libby

When the walls of the unit felt like they were closing in, Libby forced herself to go for a walk. She often saw another mother rocking a pram down by the river. One morning, when the baby was screaming, Libby walked towards her. The woman looked exhausted. She jiggled the pram back and forth, but the crying became louder. Libby smiled. It was reassuring to see someone else having trouble. 'Hello,' Libby said. The woman nodded as Libby stopped. 'Judy?' she asked. The woman looked puzzled. 'Remember me,' Libby continued, 'from the yoga class?'

'Of course, Linda wasn't it? You'll have to excuse me. I'm so tired I can hardly see straight.'

'That's okay. It's actually Libby.'

'Pardon?'

'My name, it's Libby.'

'Of course, Libby with the interesting leggings and windcheaters. How's the sewing going?'

'What do you think?' They laughed. 'How about you?' Libby asked. 'Getting any sleep?'

'Not much.'

Libby grinned. 'I know the feeling. What did you have, a boy or girl?'

'A boy.' She turned the pram so that Libby could see

inside. 'He's got a loud voice, just like his dad! How about you?'

'A girl. She's called Daniella.'

Judy peered into the pram. 'That's nice. Did you choose the name or your partner?'

'Umm, me I guess.' Libby was deliberately vague; the last thing she wanted to talk about was Darren.

'When was she born?

'Twenty-second of January. A few days early.'

'You're lucky. Zac was late. He was due on Australia Day, but he didn't arrive until the first of February.'

'How was the birth?'

Judy lifted her eyebrows. 'Not what I was expecting, but he was worth the effort. How about you?'

'Same.' They shared birth stories and Judy asked if Libby had heard from the others in their yoga class. Libby shook her head.

'Are you going to Shanti's postnatal sessions?'

'I didn't know she did postnatal classes.'

'I went last week. They're at the community centre. They have a great creche. Chelsea was there last week. She had a girl. Georgia, I think she called her.'

They talked for ages until Libby stood up reluctantly. 'It's been great catching up with you,' she said, 'but I have to go. I've got an appointment at ten. My mother's minding Daniella while I have my hair trimmed.'

'What a pity, just when I've got Zac quiet.' Judy nodded to the pram.

'I come down here most mornings,' Libby said. 'Do you want to meet tomorrow?'

'That'd be great. Sometimes I think I'll go mad if I stay in the house all day.'

So it's not only me, Libby thought. She smiled. 'How about we meet here around nine?'

'Wonderful. I'll try and keep Zac awake till the last minute so we have a chance to talk.'

'Okay. See you tomorrow.'

'Bye.'

Libby hummed as she pushed her lovely pram home. After her last experience with a mothers' group, it was a relief to meet someone more like her. Now she had two things to look forward to. Half an hour's peace at the hairdresser and her meeting with Judy.

**

The hairdresser looked at Libby from beneath her platinum fringe. 'Just a trim was it?'

Libby folded the front strands of her hair onto her forehead. 'Can you trim the front to make a fringe? The side bits keep flopping into my eyes. It's driving me mad.'

'Okay.' Libby watched her reflection as the girl began cutting. The fluoro lights made her look pale.

'Is that enough?' the hairdresser asked. Libby nodded. She didn't much care how she looked at the moment. As long as it was practical. The hairdresser was blabbing on about the latest styles, but Libby ignored her. She didn't want to be a slob, but keeping up with trends didn't seem important any more.

'Hold on a moment,' Libby said, making a sudden decision. 'Why don't you cut it all off?'

'Pardon?'

'Short. Can you cut it all short? Not just the fringe.'

The girl's eyes lit up at the prospect. Cutting long

hair short was a treat that rarely ventured into this blue-rinse-pensioners' salon. 'Are you sure?' she asked. Libby nodded. There was no one waiting so they looked through magazines of disdainful models.

'How about a soft bob around your shoulders? It wouldn't be as radical – give you a chance to get used to shorter hair.'

'No,' Libby replied. 'I haven't got time to curl the ends under. I want it short. Like that!' She pointed to a boyish style.

The hairdresser grinned. 'Great,' she said. 'I've always wanted to try that!' When she finished cutting, Libby shook her head and ran a hand through the stubble. It felt like freshly mown lawn in summer.

'Wow!' her mum said when she returned to collect Daniella. 'You look amazing.'

'Do you like it?' Libby asked.

'I'm not sure. It's different. I'm used to your hair being long.'

'It feels great. And it won't fall into the nappy bucket now!' They laughed and watched Daniella kick her chubby legs in the air.

**

Libby met Judy the next day, and the day after that. They lived so close that it was easy to pop round for a cuppa. Judy's parents lived in England and her other friends worked. They were both housebound so it made sense to spend time together. For Libby it was a relief to talk to another mother about her Daniella worries. She told Judy about the mothers' group she'd been to.

'Why don't we start our own group?' Judy suggested. 'For younger mums. People like us. We could meet once a week.'

'What if we don't like the people who turn up?'

'We could have a picnic at the park to start with. If they don't feel right we don't have to meet them again.'

'Okay,' Libby agreed. 'We could put a flyer on the health shop noticeboard.'

'Good idea. Here's a pen. Let's rough out what it should say.'

'Let's keep it simple. How about …'

Any mums (<25 years) who'd like to meet other young mothers, give Libby or Judy a call on the numbers below.

'What do you think?'

'Sounds good, but maybe it needs a heading. How about …'

Calling all Young Mums
If you're under 25 and would like to meet
other young mums, why not give Libby or
Judy a call on the numbers below.

'Yeah, that's better,' Libby said. 'I wonder how many will ring.'

They waited a week, but there was only one response. It was from a girl called Tess. She was nineteen and had just had a baby girl. Tess lived in the flats around the corner and was trying to get back into shape. 'No one told me tummies don't bounce back,' she moaned. 'After Hannah was born I still looked five months pregnant.' Tess suggested they push their prams along the cycle path as they talked, instead of sitting around on the benches. Libby and Judy liked the idea, so twice a week they met to power walk beside the river.

Week 10: Beth

Beth kicked her feet free from the doona and scratched her back. It was covered in sweat. She felt hot then clammy as she tried to grasp the fleeting mood of her dream. Something about rushing to catch a train, dropping her luggage, and looking for something she'd left behind. Beth sat up and checked the clock. Three fifteen. Strange ratty sounds scratched at the melamine walls. Was there someone in the flat? Had Sally locked herself out again? No, she was staying at her boyfriend's. Beth stared into the shadows and listened. She could hear snuffly rodent-like sounds. And there was a tap dripping somewhere. Upstairs perhaps?

A baby was crying. Was it her baby? She looked for the bassinette. Then the crying stopped and she realised it was a dream. Had she fallen asleep again? Or was it her making snuffly rodent sounds.

Jacinta had phoned before Beth went to bed. She'd told Beth about the meeting with her birth mother and Beth had suspected thoughts about the abortion would follow. She'd pushed them away, but they'd crept closer. Like hazy moonshadows they shifted, following the clouds. An occasional car sped by, otherwise the street was quiet. Beth lay back. It was time to tackle her memories.

She remembered that night, months ago, when

Marina's face had floated above her bed. Beth wondered whether Marina was okay. Then she tried to picture herself cuddling a baby. Inhaling its soft, milky smell. For a moment she glimpsed something. A chubby hand, tiny feet. A baby with turquoise, Indian Ocean eyes and combed-over-the-top curls. But then it was gone. The frustrating, not-quite-understanding tree house feeling swept over her, and suddenly it was Beth that was whimpering. There was no baby. Not any more. Sobs racked her thin body, but it was a relief to cry. Beth knew the tears had to come. It was like her other dream. The one about a wave, huge and green, which was about to engulf her. Only this time she couldn't run. The wave was dumping her onto the sand.

Beth turned on her bedside lamp and looked at herself in the mirror. Past the hazel flecks and into the black pupils of her eyes. 'It was my decision. I made the right choice,' she whispered, wondering why it was hard to hold her own gaze. She padded into the kitchen to make a cup of coffee. As the kettle boiled she thought about Jacinta and her birth mother. It had been a strange phone call. Jacinta said she didn't feel an instant connection. There were no dramatic tears and hugs. Her birth mother wore a conservative skirt and jacket. She was smaller than Jacinta expected and she kept saying how happy she was that they could meet at last, but she looked sad as she said it. Jacinta told Beth it was like meeting an old family friend. They were strangers, but Jacinta felt like she knew her. Although the meeting was an anticlimax, afterwards she kept thinking about their similarities.

'She didn't look like me,' Jacinta said, 'but it was weird, our hands are identical, and we even move them the same way. You know how I fiddle with my hair when I'm nervous?' Beth didn't but she nodded. 'Well, she does exactly the same thing!'

'Will you meet her again?'

'Mmm, she wants me to visit her house next week. I rang my parents. Dad's not happy but Mum was great. She said they were proud of me and that they'd support whatever I choose to do.' Jacinta paused. 'They'll always be my real parents, but maybe Jenny and I will become closer after a few meetings.'

'Remember what we talked about on the verandah that night?' Beth asked. 'Do you still feel the same? Would you terminate a baby if you got pregnant by accident?'

Jacinta was quiet at her end of the line. 'Yes,' she said. 'Meeting my birth mother hasn't changed how I feel. Don't get me wrong. I'm glad she didn't terminate me. I enjoy being alive, but if I wasn't, how would I know? I still feel the same as you. I've been lucky, but some kids aren't. Knowing that you weren't wanted is the worst thing. It tore me apart when I was ten.'

Beth put on her dressing-gown and poured the coffee. She savoured the bitter taste and realised that she was tired of punishing herself. 'Enough guilt!' she muttered. She found some chocolate in the pantry and took it onto the verandah. As Beth sucked caramel centres and sipped coffee, she watched clouds shroud the moon. Perhaps if she gave the embryo, Danni, her full attention, she'd be able to let it go.

Beth closed her eyes and remembered that pink heart she'd visualised in the tree house. It was beating quickly as she cradled it in her hands. 'Maybe it was selfish,' Beth whispered, 'but I wasn't ready to be your mum. I'm too young. I would have done a dreadful job, and I couldn't bear that, not when things between me and my own mum have been so good. And the other choice, giving a baby up for adoption, I couldn't do that either. Kids need unconditional love. My child would be my responsibility. I couldn't pass that on to a stranger. I'm sorry, Danni, I couldn't let you grow into a child. I hope you understand, and also ... if you can, please forgive me.' Beth watched the heartbeat falter and fade. Then she saw Danni melt into a clump of soft, feathery wings, which paused, then drifted out of her pelvis into the sky.

Beth held the warm mug of coffee to her face and tears streamed along her cheeks. A huge feeling of relief replaced the bitterness of guilt. Danni had gone. Beth sighed and felt a long-forgotten sense of peace and tranquillity drift over her.

Week 11: Libby

Libby smeared jaffa-red lipstick into a pout shape. Then she stood back and smiled. Bright, just what she wanted. She dressed Daniella and went to meet Judy and Tess at the park.

'I've decided to have Daniella baptised,' Libby announced as they walked along the foreshore.

'Are you sure? I thought you said you could better appreciate God by the river. Without the glitzy trimmings, I think you said.'

Libby nodded. 'I did, but the church has been such an important part of my life. I don't want Daniella to miss out on that.'

'So you'll be going to mass again?'

'Probably. I thought about it last night when I was feeding her. Perhaps it was divine intervention,' Libby laughed. 'But I really want Daniella to be baptised, so she can be a member of our church. If she chooses to pray by the river when she's older, that's fine with me.'

'Your mother will be happy.'

'Mmm.'

'What about your dad?'

'Who knows? I'm tempted to not tell him.'

'That wouldn't be fair.'

'What!'

'For Daniella. If she's going to be baptised, he should be there.'

'He hasn't been very supportive.'

'I know, but that's your fight, not Daniella's. Having grandparents is too important to stuff up. I know, I missed out because my parents wouldn't talk to their parents.'

'Hmm. I'll have to think about that. Anyway, I've decided to make Daniella a fantastic christening gown.'

'Aha, so that's the reason.'

Libby laughed. 'Maybe I just need an excuse to dress her up and have a party.' They rested under a tree while Judy reorganised Zac's nappy. 'I don't s'pose either of you knows anyone with a sewing machine that smocks?' Libby asked. Her friends shook their heads.

'Don't you have one at home?'

'Grandma left me her old machine, but I'd love one that does smocking. I've got this detailed pattern in mind for Daniella's dress. I could do the smocking by hand, but it'd take twice as long.'

'If I win lotto this weekend, I'll buy you one. How much are they?'

'You can sometimes get them second-hand. Brand new they cost a fortune.'

**

'Hey, Libby, there's a sewing machine down at Cash Converters,' Tess panted as Libby opened the door to her brisk knocking. 'I asked the bloke whether it does smocking. He reckons he'd have to read the instructions, but he thinks so.'

'How much is it?'

'Three hundred and fifty.'

'That's cheap if it does smocking, but it's three hundred and fifty more than I have.'

'You could look at it as a business investment. I was telling my cousin about Daniella's gown. She wants to know how much you'd charge to do one for her.'

'She could borrow Daniella's after the baptism if she wants to.'

'Are you crazy? Martina married a dermatologist. They're rolling in money, and they're planning a big family. She'd want an outfit she could use again.'

'I wouldn't know what to charge.'

'Well, I've seen them in the shops for over two hundred. But they aren't as nice as Daniella's will be.'

'Would she buy the fabric herself?'

'No. She's too busy with the baby. She wants someone to organise it all for her. Any spare time she has is spent helping out at the clinic.'

'When's the christening?'

'In three weeks.'

'I'd never make it in time. I have to finish Daniella's first.'

'If you bought the machine, you'd easily do it. I can mind Daniella for a few hours if you like.'

Libby smiled. 'That's nice, but I still haven't got three hundred and fifty dollars.'

'You could ask your mum.'

Libby raised her eyebrows. 'I don't think so.'

'Well, I could put it on my bankcard. Then you could pay me after my cousin pays you.'

'No, I can't.'

'Why not?'

'I don't want to owe you money.'

'It would only be for a while. You could make

Hannah some clothes as part payment and after a few pensions, it'll be paid off.' Tess could see Libby was tempted. 'Why don't you go and have a look? It might not be the right kind anyway.'

'They've probably sold it by now. That's really cheap for a machine that smocks.'

'They'll still have it. I asked the man to hold it until tomorrow.'

'You don't take no for an answer, do you?'

'Not often,' Tess grinned, before sniffing Hannah's bottom. 'You need a change,' she told her daughter.

**

'If you want to do this sewing thing, then of course I'll lend you the money for the machine,' Libby's mum said when she popped in after work with some lemons.

'How do you know about it?' Libby asked.

'I saw your friend Tess at the deli. You know Grandma left me some money. I'd like to give it to you, but you can think of it as a loan and pay it back some day if you prefer.'

'But why? I thought you wanted me to get back into music.'

'I'd rather you went back to your cello, but if you want to sew instead ...'

Gail produced a bottle of wine and a corkscrew. She pulled the cork and poured them both a glass. 'You know, you never asked me why I gave up my music.'

'Yes I did. You said you met Dad and decided to have babies.' It was hard for Libby to not sound judgemental.

'Yes, but there was more to it than that. You were born the same year we were married. Haven't you ever wondered about that?'

Libby was puzzled. 'I don't understand.'

Gail sighed. 'I've dropped hints, but you've been a bit slow. I married your father because I was pregnant. Pregnant with you.'

'But ... No!' Libby cried, suddenly understanding. Her face crumpled. 'Then you gave up your music because of me,' she whispered.

Gail nodded. 'In those days mothers didn't have much choice. You were born before the supporting mother's pension.'

'But why didn't you go back to your music later?'

'I played the piano after you were born, but then James came along.' Gail shrugged. 'It was just too difficult. You wanted my attention when he slept and it was hard to play when you were both awake. I didn't have time to practise. You know how it is with an instrument. Once you stop practising ...'

'Why didn't you tell me this before?'

Gail sipped her wine. 'The time never seemed right,' she said.

**

Libby woke early. She'd barely slept. All night she kept thinking about her mother. How she'd misjudged her. Daniella was gurgling happily in her bassinette. Libby kissed her and breathed in her delicious baby smell. It was a beautiful morning with a warm autumn breeze. Libby decided to take Daniella out for an early stroll. 'Look, the trees are shaking their sillies out!' she said, pointing to the palms. Daniella looked up with a serious expression and put her thumb in her mouth.

'Yes, you're right,' Libby muttered. 'Mummy needs more adult company. I might ring Ashleigh and see if she has time to visit.'

She strode along the foreshore, listening to the water slap the limestone bricks. The Tai Chi group was in full swing. Libby envied their calm as she tucked a rug around Daniella's knees. She walked and walked. Her mind was buzzing and she felt more alive than she had in weeks. Daniella fell asleep but still Libby walked. It was like deja vu. She was following her mother's path. But it wasn't the same. Libby had a choice.

She crossed Mounts Bay Road and pushed the stroller into Kings Park. The world had spun thousands of times since her birth. Things had happened. Women had struggled. There were options now. It was a shame that Daniella wouldn't have a daddy, but maybe her own father would mellow. She could still do her music part time. Gail had offered to baby-sit, and if studying became too hard, she could sew christening gowns for a few years. Start a small business until Daniella was at kindy.

Libby power walked the pram until she reached the café near the tennis courts. She ordered a coffee and sat at a table. Leaning back, Libby watched seagulls kamikaze through thermals as fluffy clouds covered the sun. It was hard to see into the glare, but Libby knew there were silver linings up there somewhere. Some days you just had to look harder.

As she walked home Libby saw two boys flying kites by the foreshore. 'Look, Daniella,' she said as the wind snip-snapped the plastic dragons. Daniella gurgled and Libby remembered the day last October when she'd held the jellyfish kite. It seemed such a long time ago.

Things would be okay. She would make them okay.

Libby watched a family picnicking by the playground. Three generations squabbling below the seagulls. She knew it was important to give her daughter the same opportunities she'd had. Having her baptised was a first step, but Daniella would need a godmother and godfather. She wondered if her parents would agree. Her mum would probably jump at the chance to nudge another soul along the true path. She could even patch the areas where she'd gone wrong with Libby. Her father would be harder to convince. First she'd have to get him to talk to her.

Libby turned the pram towards home. James would be at his scout camp. Her parents would be alone. It was now or never. The worst they could do was refuse.

Libby went inside and rang her old phone number. Her father answered. 'Hi, Dad,' she said. 'I was wondering if you and Mum would like to come over for dinner tonight. I've decided to have Daniella baptised, but I wanted to talk to you and Mum first. Hear what you think.' Libby could feel her father's hesitation, so she rushed on. 'I thought I'd try and do roast lamb.' Libby knew roast was his favourite. She held her breath, wondering if he realised how hard this was for her. 'I would really like you both to come.'

'Hmm,' Jim replied awkwardly. 'I'll have to check with your mother, but it sounds … nice. What time do you want us there?' As she cradled the phone Libby tried to make sense of her feelings. He was the one who'd been pig-headed. But even though she felt right, Libby guessed that it was hard for her dad, too. Becoming a parent was changing the way she looked at things. It would be nice to talk to him again. They'd always been so similar.

Week 12: Beth

Beth was heading for the library when she saw him. He was walking with another guy. She hesitated, remembering the last time they'd spoken at the school presentation ceremony. Then Darren turned and saw her. 'Beth, I was hoping I'd run into you sometime.'

'Hi, Darren. How's science going?'

'Pretty boring so far. How about you? You obviously got into music,' he said, nodding towards her cello case. 'How's it going?'

'Good,' Beth answered. 'There are two others doing cello, and I've started flute too.'

'Great.'

'And you? What did you decide to major in?'

'Marine Biology. The first units aren't very interesting, but supposedly it gets better.'

The other fellow smiled and held out his hand. 'I'm Rhett,' he said.

'Oh, sorry,' Darren apologised. 'Rhett, this is Beth. We were … at school together.'

'Are you studying science too?'

Rhett nodded. 'Same basics as Darren, but I want to specialise in coastal management.'

'That sounds interesting. I love the beach. It's where I go to think,' Beth replied, before turning back to Darren. 'Did you end up doing philosophy?' she asked.

'Yeah, it's my favourite subject. I'm wondering whether I should have taken an arts degree instead.'

'Your father would have loved that! How's Sasha?' The words popped out, but as she waited for him to reply Beth realised that she wasn't jealous any more. In fact she hoped they were happy. She remembered the image of soft wings flying into the night and smiled. The girl who'd followed them around last year had gone. It was a weird feeling.

'She's okay, but finding Year Twelve different from Year Eleven,' he laughed. 'Aren't you glad that's over?'

Beth nodded. She could feel Rhett watching her. 'So, how many sporting teams have you joined?' she asked Darren.

'Just water polo and rowing, but I might start hockey in a few weeks. How about you?'

'I'm thinking about joining the Buddhist group. I went to a meeting in O-week and it was really interesting.'

'Do your mum and dad know?'

Beth shook her head. 'I want to see if I like it before dropping any bombshells.'

'I went to a few sessions in Fremantle,' Rhett interrupted. 'My sister's really into it.' Beth turned to Rhett. He and Darren were male versions of Snow White and Rose Red, both good-looking, but in different ways. 'Maybe we could meet for coffee one afternoon,' Rhett continued, 'and I could introduce her to you.'

Darren didn't seem too keen on the idea, but Beth smiled. 'That'd be nice,' she said.

Week 13: Libby

After the blessing, Jim took the little bundle in his arms. 'Now you're part of our church,' he said. Daniella opened her eyes to stare at him and Jim felt there was a connection. This little mite knew he was her grandad. She smiled, burped quietly and went to sleep. Gail watched her husband thaw. 'She's a cutie isn't she?' Gail whispered. Jim hesitated. He didn't want to give in that easily. Someone had to impose standards. There was an issue here. He'd been right to stick to his guns. Then he looked across at his daughter's face. Libby was anxious, but she hid it well. Jim caught a glimpse of his princess, then she was gone, as Libby adjusted her strong mother mask back into place. He watched her thanking Father Patrick and wondered whether he'd been right to push her away.

What else could he have done? She'd had no idea of the responsibilities of becoming a parent. Perhaps she still didn't. Surely it had been his duty to protect her. To try and convince her to give up the child. To hang onto her dreams and aspirations. Not to have to marry Darren. But his plan hadn't worked and, as he looked down at Daniella again, Jim realised that he might have been wrong. Libby was a mother now, but somewhere deeper she was still his little girl. As he held Libby's child, Jim realised with surprise that he was proud of her. Libby was brave. She'd always been brave, but she was vulnerable too. And now there was this babe. She shared his blood and it was obvious they'd be needing him now that Darren-the-no-hoper had shirked his responsibilities.

'Not like me,' he muttered. Jim kissed Daniella's hair. Poor little mite. She'll need her grandad to help look after her. 'Don't you worry,' he told her, 'I'll be here to watch out for you.'

Libby walked over and asked if he wanted her to take Daniella. 'She's all right,' he growled. 'We're getting to know each other.'

Libby smiled. 'She seems happy with you,' she said shyly.

'Mmm, I haven't lost my touch.'

Gail rearranged the bunny-rug. 'She's perfect, isn't she?'

Jim nodded. 'That she is,' he whispered, thanking God for showing him the path to compassion. 'She's a tiny angel from God,' he said, 'come to join our family.' Daniella puckered her face into a frown and howled her agreement.

'Sounds like it's time for a feed,' Libby said. Gail squeezed Libby's hand. Her daughter was a woman. There were rifts, but they were learning to step carefully. They'd come through the worst and they were still a family. That was the important thing. Somehow they'd be okay.

James looked on with amusement. Everyone was making a fuss over the little prune, but he didn't mind. She was quite cute and, for the first time since Libby got into trouble, they were acting like a family again. It was funny to watch how soppy grown-ups could be —even Libby. But at least no one was yelling. Well, no one except Daniella anyway.

Beth stared at the phone and wondered whether to return Rhett's call. She pushed the answering machine button and listened to his message for the third time.

> *Hi Beth, it's Rhett. Thought I'd call and see if you want to meet in Freo. There's a good movie opening the weekend after next. It's pretty deep, so it should fit in well with your philosophy unit. We could stop at my sister's place after the show, and she can tell you about the Buddhism classes. Hopefully I'll bump into you at uni next week, but if not, why don't you call me? I'd really like to hear from you. See you.*

Beth smiled. He had a nice voice. She sat back to think about Rhett, but Darren's face kept interrupting.

'Go away. I'm over you,' she told the face.

'Are you sure?' It looked wistful, like the old Darren. The one who'd waited for her under the tree that day. 'Maybe we could try again,' it whispered.

'No! What we had was nice, but it would never have lasted.'

'How do you know?'

'Oh, Darren, I just do. We're too different.'

'Opposites attract.'

'Not us!'

The face frowned. 'Are you sure it was right though, not to try …'

'We've been through this before. You would've hated being stuck with me and a baby. And I would've hated it too. We would have fought.' Beth shuddered. She knew they'd have dragged each other down. Bringing a child into that kind of mess wouldn't have been right for either of them. 'It's better this way,' she said.

'But what about your faith?' the Darren face asked. 'I wanted to talk to you about that, but you wouldn't answer the phone and you kept avoiding me.' Beth thought about Father Patrick and what she believed.

'The church teachings are okay in an ideal world,' she whispered, 'but this world isn't ideal. I keep thinking about all those unwanted babies. You know, the orphans and abandoned kids in overcrowded institutions, babies dying of AIDS in third world countries. Death is an ordinary part of life in many communities. They don't have time for guilt.'

'But we don't live in a country like that …'

Beth chewed her lip. 'No, but I still don't think it's responsible to bring another unwanted child into the world.' The Darren face looked sceptical as it faded away, but Beth shrugged. The life she'd chosen to terminate was a developing cell mass, a potential baby, but not yet a baby. If the church she loved called that murder, well, she'd have to live with that. She remembered the night on her balcony. Had she imagined the feathery image to soothe her conscience? She closed her eyes and the vision of wings returned. A warm feeling spread across her body. She knew her child's spirit had forgiven her. It was time to move on.

Beth pushed the message button again. Then she took a deep breath and picked up the phone. 'Hello,' Rhett answered.

'Hi,' Beth said. 'The movie idea sounds great. What time do you want to meet?'

Week 15: Libby

Libby stared at her reflection in the mirror. After last week's yoga class, Shanti suggested they study their eyes during a quiet moment. 'Accept whatever you find there,' she'd said. 'Acceptance is the first step towards change. If you want to share your feelings, we can talk about them during the next class.'

It was harder than it sounded. Libby felt silly, then embarrassed. She wondered why. There was no one watching. Only herself. She looked away, then tried again. What did she see there? Libby wasn't sure. A brave mask covering something. She didn't know what.

The doorbell rang and Libby glanced at her watch. Her dad was as punctual as ever. He was taking them out for lunch at his club. Libby knew that going public with them was hard for him. 'Can I come in?' Jim called, opening the door. He handed Libby a bunch of flowers and tiptoed over to Daniella's pram. 'How's my princess?' he asked.

'Sleeping!'

'I meant the other one.'

Libby turned in surprise. She smiled. 'I'm fine thanks, Dad,' she said quietly.

'Right, well then the others are in the car,' Jim said gruffly. 'Better rattle your dags, girl, or we'll be late.'

'If you take the pram, I'll lock up and be there in a minute.' After he'd gone, Libby looked into the mirror, tousled her hair and rolled on some lip gloss. She smiled at her father's words and knew she'd made the right choice. Her path wouldn't be easy, but she was a wiser princess now. She grabbed her bag, locked the door, and wondered what kind of crown to wear today.

Week 16: Beth

Beth gazed at her reflection in the mirror. Ashleigh had read about this activity where you stare into your own eyes. 'Mirrors reflect how we feel about ourselves,' she'd said. 'Look at yourself and try to say something nice. It feels really weird, but it's s'posed to be good for you.'

It did feel weird, and it was harder than it sounded. Beth felt silly, then embarrassed. She wondered why. There was no one watching. Only herself. She looked away, then tried again. What did she see there? Beth wasn't sure. Despite all those philosophy questions, there was still a lot to learn, but maybe that's what life was about.

The doorbell rang and Beth glanced at her watch. Rhett was early. They'd decided to go to his sister's house before the movie, then on to a café after the show. Beth turned away from the mirror and hesitated. Rhett was nice, but after the Victor thing she wanted to go slowly. Beth needed space before she began the next round of mistakes.

'Can I come in?' Rhett called, opening the door. He kissed her lightly on the cheek.

'You should keep it locked,' Rhett said. 'Strangers might get in.' Was he teasing, or flirting? Beth wasn't sure, but her cheek tingled.

'Would you like coffee?' she asked.

'No, I'm double-parked.'

'Okay, I'll lock up and be down in a minute.' After he'd gone, Beth checked her reflection once more. She hummed Pachelbel's canon and smiled as she tousled her hair and smudged red gloss over her lips. As she walked towards the car, Beth dragged her feelings into perspective. She thought about relinquished mothers, divorced mums, mothers of stillborn babies. Indulging her own sadness seemed trivial in comparison. She knew she'd made the right choice for her. Danni had forgiven her. That was all. It was time to let go.

Beth took a deep breath and smiled at Rhett. 'Ready when you are,' she said, opening the door.